Death Takes A Break

A Taylor Texas Mystery

Morewellson, Ltd.

Death Takes A Break

Copyright @ 2019 by Vikki Walton

For permission requests, write to the publisher:
Attention: Permissions Coordinator
Morewellson, Ltd.
P. O. Box 49726

Colorado Springs, Colorado 80949-9726

ISBN:
978-1-950452-12-5 (standard edition print)
978-1-950452-11-8 (e-pub)
978-1-950452-13-2 (large print edition)

This is a work of fiction. Names characters, places and incidents either are the product of the author's imagination or are used fictitiously, and any resemblance to actual persons, living or dead, business establishments, events, or locales is entirely coincidental. In order to provide a sense of place for the story, business establishment names have been included under the aspect of "nominative fair use" of products or services. No establishment noted in this fictional account has provided any incentive or endorsement of said account.

Front cover illustration: Mariah Sinclair
Publishing/design services: Wild Seas Formatting
(http://www.WildSeasFormatting.com)
Editing: Top Shelf editing services

Death Takes A Break
A Taylor Texas Mystery
Morewellson, Ltd.

Chapter One

There's no mistaking the sound of a shotgun being engaged.

Cha-chuck.

Christie sat bolt upright and sought the source of the noise. Nothing she could see with a quick glance around. She struggled to unwrap the sheet tangled around her from in the night while she slept on the rust-colored tweed sofa. Oblivious to the fact that she only wore an extra-long Cowboys jersey, she scrambled over to the open front door. Peeking around the corner, she saw her father, R.C., with his shotgun at his side. It pointed to the ground and her Pop's finger was off the trigger.

Looking toward the driveway, a man stood on the packed earth leading up to the porch. Pushing the auburn curls from her face, Christie subconsciously tucked the hair behind her ear. A sound caught her attention. Glancing to her right, she saw her father's dogs, Mutt and Jeffrey laying on the porch, their heads moving back and forth between Pop and the stranger. As they did so, their tails went up and down in a half-hearted attempt between being friendly and hesitation. The rescued labs were good dogs but weren't much use as guard dogs. People really had to be bad for them to bark at them.

Christie's attention returned to the man as her father spoke. "You can tell that no-account boss of yours that my answer's the same. I ain't selling my property and that's final."

Selling the property? Pop had said nothing to her about that. Christie moved closer and the man's head swiveled over to where she stood behind the screen door.

"Christie, come on out here," her father intoned.

She opened the screen door but stayed inside. The man pushed his lips together, bowed his head and looked at the ground. Embarrassed, she realized she had been standing there in the skimpy top.

As a hospice nurse, Christie had seen and heard almost everything possible, but appearing half-naked to a stranger wasn't a great way to start the morning.

"Just a minute, Pop."

She hurried back inside and grabbed the blue jeans she'd shucked off on the leather recliner before going to bed. She didn't want to leave Pop for too long, so she shrugged into her denim jacket that she'd tossed nearby, crossed her arms over her ample chest and elbowed the door open.

"What's going on? Pop, put down that shotgun before someone gets hurt."

"That's the point of a shotgun, Missy." He turned back to the man. "Now git off my property."

Christie stifled the sigh that sought to escape her lips. To her knowledge, the only time her father had shot the gun was when he killed a rattler and that had been decades ago.

The young Hispanic man wore the prerequisite Texas men's outfit of a crisp white shirt, starched blue jeans, and much-worn cowboy boots. The only noticeable difference is that he wore a straw hat over a baseball cap or felt hat. His shirt was embroidered above the pocket with a company logo. While Christie struggled to read the business tag, he'd stayed far enough back from the porch to make a quick return to his truck. He'd parked so it was also difficult to see the firm's name on the side of his dually cab.

"Ma'am," he removed his sunglasses. "Are you his daughter? I'm here to speak with your father about a great opportunity he has with this land. As you may know, Boerne is growing so quickly that they can't keep up with the pace and it's just a matter of time before people want to seek property further out. To put it bluntly, your father stands to make millions with all this acreage. And he'd still get to keep a parcel, should he want it–like this homestead, for example."

Pop grumbled, "Well, ain't that mighty generous that I'd get to keep land that's been in my family for generations."

"Sir, I meant no disrespect—"

R.C. Taylor took a step toward the porch railing and spat, "Y'all destroyed places that have been in families for generations with all your development. I won't have you come ruining it here too."

Christie stepped forward and laid her hand on her dad's arm. She addressed the man. "Mister—"

"Garcia. Hector Garcia." He tipped his hat and Christie got a glimpse of a full head of thick wavy black hair.

"Mr. Garcia. I haven't heard about any of this as I just arrived last night, but I'll speak to my father, okay?" Christie knew her father had no intention of selling the property, but she wanted a chance to speak to him alone. She figured this would end the current conversation and calm her father down.

"Certainly." He pulled a business card from his pocket and Mutt raised his head as if to show he was on the job. Hector took one step toward the porch before appearing to change his mind about it.

Christie came off the porch and retrieved the

business card from him. "Thanks. We'll let you know."

He tipped his hat and turned so that his head was away from R.C. Under his breath, Hector said, "This is a great opportunity. Your dad's not getting younger and all that money would go to you on his passing."

Christie flinched. She wanted to say, "Are you kidding me?" Instead, she pressed her lips together and stuffed his card in her jacket pocket. Striding confidently to the truck, he swung up into the cab in one easy movement. Hector started the truck up, touching a finger to his hat in a gesture of politeness seen all over Texas.

Christie stepped back into the shade of the front porch as the man reversed the truck, kicking up dust. The dogs jumped off the porch, barking excitedly as the truck made its way down the drive.

"Now you're tough guys?" Christie threw back her head and laughed. They ran up to her and Christie petted their heads as they fought each other for her attention, tails wagging and tongues lolling with enthusiasm. "You're absolutely worthless, you know." The labs seemed to smile at her as they followed her to the porch where Pop now sat in a rocker, the shotgun open and resting on his knees.

"Pop, give me that before you shoot your foot off."

"Not my eye out?" he grinned and winked at her.

"Funny. Not." But she still smiled at his corny humor attempt.

"Ah, it's not loaded, darling."

Tears sprung to her eyes at the old familiar nickname. She'd been known by her last name—Taylor—for so long that even going by Christie again would take some getting used to hearing. Now the sound of her Pop's endearment for her felt like a sweet caress. While at home, she'd enjoy being called by her first name again. Maybe that would be another way to erase some of her past hurts and the reason she'd returned to Comfort, Texas and the old homestead.

Her thoughts traveled back to that horrible

weekend when tragedy had struck her and some old college friends. Being stuck in a blizzard with someone who was a killer had made her realize that she had grown tired of being around misery and death constantly. The idea of not knowing when your life would end had made her think twice about her current position and life's trajectory. While she had dealt with the aftermath of her feelings about the weekend and all that had occurred, going back to work at the hospice center had taken its toll on her. She couldn't give her patients the care they needed when she was burnt out.

Realizing how much of a toll it had taken on her, she'd asked for leave and management graciously told her to take all the time she needed, that a place would be there whenever she wanted to come back. Even though dealing with death had been a daily part of her job it had never caused her the angst that had crippled her work. Natural death was difficult enough without someone who sought to cause harm being a part of your life. It had made her think back to some of her patients.

Had they died natural deaths, or had they been 'helped along' in death? The thought that she may have missed those signs weighed her down mentally and emotionally.

During her years of care, she often received notes of appreciation from patients and their families remarking that her sweet spirit had been a great comfort as they said their final goodbyes. Yet, when an old college friend had been murdered, something snapped. Her heart had broken and for the first time, she realized that her work was suffering because of it. She needed time away from death. Time for life so she'd done the best thing she knew to do. She needed comfort.

She'd come home.

Pop reached over and Christie placed her hand in his arthritic scarred one. He squeezed her hand, but the firm grip she recalled from her youth wasn't there.

A moment of silence passed between them.

She patted her father's hand. "How's about some of your homemade biscuits?"

"That sounds mighty good. We can do a fry-up." He struggled to rise from his chair, and it was at that moment that Christie saw the frail, old man her father had become. The rolled-up sleeves of his flannel shirt showed arms peppered with bruises on reddened skin. She took the gun from him and cocked it over her left arm. With her right hand, she offered him help to stand up from the chair. Shooing her hand away, he reached up and smoothed down his sparse, gray hair. As he moved, he stumbled but quickly regained his footing.

She reached over to help him. Christie had never been a petite girl. She had used this to great benefit in her job as a nurse and she now had her own "guns"—with strong muscles on each arm. Her patients families had sometimes called her a pistol on numerous occasions when dealing with her. In private, her patients would chuckle and thank her for saying things they'd wanted to say for years. She was a strong, substantial woman who wouldn't be bullied, and proud of it.

"I'm good. I got this." He waved her off.

"Okay, Pop. You don't want to walk your baby

girl inside? Up to you."

He made a face but laced his arm through hers. Inside the house, she placed the gun back in its spot over the front door and strode through the small living area into the kitchen. Originally a small house, the home expansion over the years hadn't made it much bigger. Peeling paint, loose floorboards and other noticeable defects meant the old homestead wasn't being maintained the way it should be, and the house needed lots of repairs that have been set aside. A few window units and fans barely kept the place cool against the harsh Texas heat. It would be nice for her father to have a better place to live but she knew he'd never leave his home.

"Pop, I'm going to grab a quick shower first if that's okay."

"Sure. I'll go out and collect the eggs." He patted her cheek. "It's so nice to have you home, darling."

The shower felt good on her tight muscles after the long days she'd spent driving home. She'd forgotten how long it had been just to drive through Texas. At least now being able to do a quick pitstop at Buc-ee's had made the trip a bit more bearable. After gassing up the Jeep and grabbing a bunch of snacks for fortification for the drive ahead, she'd finally made it home late last night.

After her shower, she shucked into a tank-top, shorts and flip-flops hoping that would help keep her cooler. She heard an old country tune playing in the kitchen on the old radio. She gathered her clothes up and dumped them into a basket. Her stomach grumbled so other chores could wait until later.

The father and daughter duo worked in the kitchen in companionable silence. Using an iron skillet that had been passed down through the generations and was at least seventy years old, Christie fried up bacon and eggs, while her father made biscuits from scratch. She'd watched her mother do the same thing for many years growing up in this very house. The home, though it had been small in size, had been large with the fullness of love. Her parents had struggled with having children, but Christie had been a surprise after they'd given up.

Her mother had been the heart of their home and when she'd succumbed to breast cancer, her father had grieved her loss so much that Christie didn't know if he would ever recover. But he had a daughter to raise and so one day she had felt the shift in him back to the land of the living.

Grief was like that and Christie had seen it with so many patient's families. It took hold and you had to allow it because no matter what you did, until it let you go, you were useless in fighting it.

She smiled at her father as he bent over the bowl, pouring in just enough buttermilk to make the biscuits the right consistency. Neither he nor her mother had ever used a recipe and simply knew what amounts to add from so many times of making the golden biscuits.

After he'd put the biscuits in the oven, the old man took a bowl and went out to the backyard where beehives stood. From the kitchen window, Christie watched as he opened the cover and pulled up the frame. With his bare hand, he broke off a chunk of honeycomb and put it in the bowl before returning the frame to the hive and closing the lid.

Christie finished frying up the sausage and eggs by the time he came back inside the house. She spied red blotches on his hands as he set the bowl down. "Pop, the bees stung you." There was no point in saying he should have worn gloves or a hood. "Shouldn't you put something on it?"

"Nah. Helps my arthritis. So I get honey and medical treatment at the same time." He smiled at her. "Let's chow down. I'm hungry for once."

They sat in silence and ate. When Pop leaned back in his chair, Christie broached the subject. "Pop, what's this about selling the property? You've said nothing to me about it before."

"They've been hounding me now for neigh-on a year. The price keeps going up and up. But what's money to me? When I die, you can sell the property or pass it on to your kids." He grabbed a toothpick and picked at his tobacco-stained teeth.

Christie didn't respond. She was already in

her forties and didn't have plans for a husband, much less children at this point in her life. Some women were made to be mothers, and some women were better on their own. She'd chosen that path early in life and didn't see her viewpoint on it changing anytime soon.

He cocked an eyebrow and pointed the toothpick at her. "You need a man."

"Pop, no woman 'needs' a man. We're all very capable on our own. But let's not go down that rabbit hole. You could get a nice place, and it would meet all your needs. No worries about ..." She stopped short before saying the house was falling down around him.

"I know what'cher thinking. I admit I'm not as spry as I once was. It just takes me a bit longer to get to projects around here." He shifted in his seat. "But at least I ain't like old man Curtis. Almost burned his house down, he did." He stuck the toothpick back in his mouth and leaned back in his chair.

Christie struggled not to imagine him falling over on his back. She eyed another biscuit. "That's terrible. What happened?"

"He'd told me over coffee that he'd been forgetting where he put things. He even wondered if he was coming down with that dementia thing."

"Pop, you don't 'come down with' dementia. It's not like a cold. Why did he say that?"

"He'd go to the barn to feed the horses, and the tools were on the other side of the shed from where they ought to be. One day, he found the gates open, and the cows were up around the house. Things like that."

"Well, everyone gets forgetful sometimes. It doesn't mean his long-term memory is compromised. Has he gone to a doctor to check it out?"

"Yep. He finally did when he came home and found stuff in the fridge that shouldn't have been in there."

"What did the doctor say?"

"Said he was fine. Healthy for a man his age. No issues."

"Then what happened?" Christie grabbed a piece of the honeycomb and stuck it in her mouth, then licked her fingers.

"Well, that dern developer had been bugging Curtis to sell his place too. But Curtis wouldn't budge. The developer said that, when he went out there, Curtis took a shot at him. Curtis denied it, but when the sheriff checked his guns, sure 'nuff, his rifle had been fired. The developer agreed not to press charges if Curtis would sell him a portion of the land. Curtis told him to take that offer and stick it where the sun doesn't shine."

Christie laughed. "I can see him doing that."

Or you. Birds of a feather.

Pop stroked his scratchy, gray beard. "But the fire changed everything."

"Go on." Christie leaned her elbows on the table.

"From what they can figure, Curtis must have dropped one of his cigarettes, and the hay in the barn caught fire. Luckily, the horses were out in the field, so no harm there. A couple of the horses did have some minor injuries from sparks and getting spooked. They're being boarded at the vets while Curtis figures things out. They saved the house, but the barn's a total loss."

"Insurance should cover that." Christie saw her father swallow. "Don't tell me he didn't have insurance?"

"He was living on social security. He can't afford to have a new barn built. Unless..." He left the words unspoken.

Christie laced her fingers together. "Unless he sold some of his land. Well, that's very convenient for the developer."

"That's my girl. Exactly what I was thinking." Pop touched his forehead with his index finger.

"You don't think..."

He responded, "That someone intentionally set the fire?"

"So you do." Christie wiped her hands on a napkin and waited to hear his response.

"Well, can't be sure. But I know I wouldn't trust that developer as far as I can throw her."

Christie pushed back from the table, "Wait, did you say her? It's not Hector Garcia?"

"No. It's Emma Webster."

Why did that name sound familiar?

"She used to go to school with you. I think her

brother was in your class. Albert, I think."

Christie thought back to her class. Like many small country towns, her school had been tiny, probably twenty in her graduating class. She couldn't remember an Albert, but Emma sounded like a name she remembered.

"So, she's the developer?"

"Her and her husband. Um, Tyler's his name. Though, she runs the show. I wouldn't want to be married to that woman. Ooh-we. She's something. And it ain't good. What she wants, she gets." He leaned toward Christie as if others could overhear their conversation. "Word is, she's been having an affair with someone in town. But no one's naming names." He cocked his eyebrows and tilted his chin.

Christie chuckled. "Since when have you started listening to gossip? Seems like I remember you telling me it's not polite—"

He waved his hand at her. "I know you don't talk to no one, so it ain't spreading gossip."

"Hmm, okay." Christie motioned to his plate with most of the eggs and biscuit untouched. She reached over and took his plate. "Are you sure you're done?"

He nodded. "Harder to eat these days. Sounds good, but then," he shrugged, "it's tough getting old."

Christie changed the subject. "Maybe I should talk to her. Emma—Webster, did you say? Let her know you're not interested in selling. Would you like me to do that?"

She scraped the leftover eggs and sausage into Mutt and Jeffrey's bowls, and they immediately came running, inhaling the food with quick gulps. As Christie filled the deep farmhouse sink with hot, soapy water, she piled the stacked plates next to it on the counter.

"If it gets her to stop sending those guys out here to pester me, that'd be great. Albert, Hector, Cole."

Cole.

~~~

She hadn't heard his name in years. They say high school love is often puppy love, but it had
~~~

sure been real to this puppy. They'd hung out and spent lazy summers riding horses or swimming in the cold Guadalupe River. Over the years, they'd grown into friends. Then, one summer, Christie felt the shift in her heart. They'd agreed to meet, but Cole never showed up. Transported back to that moment, Christie recalled the feeling of betrayal as if it were yesterday. How could he have been so cruel? She'd thought she'd known him, but she'd been so wrong. She'd also lost one of her best friends.

Chapter Two

Christie had finished cleaning the dishes when her cell phone ringing brought her back to the present. She picked it up and glanced at the number. It didn't look familiar. She answered with a hesitant "hello?"

"Christie!"

"Trish. Oh, my gosh. How long has it been?"

"Too long."

"I'm so glad to hear from you." Christie wiped her hands with a dishcloth and moved out to the front porch and took a seat in the rocker. She stretched back and put her feet up on the porch's banister. "What have you been up to? Other than trying to save some animal."

Lighthearted laughter came through the phone. "You still know me. My husband says he'll disown me if I bring one more stray home."

"I doubt that. If I recall, he worships the

ground you walk on." She swatted at a mosquito the size of a cow. *Welcome back to Texas where everything's bigger.*

Christie went back inside. Pop sat in his recliner, already asleep and snoring softly so she went back into the kitchen.

"Maybe not as much as when we were in school, but," Trish giggled again, "okay, he does. I got lucky."

"Yes, you did." Christie remembered how the girls had gone their separate ways once boys came into the picture. They'd remained friends, but whereas Trish had stuck to her roots, Christie had dived into medical textbooks, determined to become a doctor. She'd planned on going to UTSA in San Antonio, but when word went around that another friend, Kimberly was dating Cole, she applied to schools out of state. With her grades, several good schools accepted her. She'd chosen one far away from the small town and away from the heartache.

She switched ears, trying to hear better. "Hey, if I lose you, it's because of poor service out here.

Pop still lives in the stone age with internet. How did you get my number?"

"I called my daddy, who called your Pop and got the number. Oh, Christie, it's been so long. When can we meet up?"

"My calendar's pretty free. You let me know."

Silence came over the line before Trish responded. "How's about a late lunch today over at Bumdoodlers? I know you love their pie."

"Sounds good to me. How about 1:30?"

"Great. That gives me plenty of time before I have to head over to the school to pick up Jess after practice. You coming to the game?"

It was like she'd never stepped away. Fridays were always reserved for hometown football. Christie and Trish had spent Saturdays tubing on the river and Sundays found them in the pew, trying not to think about the aromas from the pot-luck spread waiting for after the sermon con-cluded. Small-town life couldn't be beat when it came to a comforting consistency.

"Let me think about it. I've just come back for a short visit, so I want to spend some time with

Pop."

"Okay. He's welcome to come, too."

"You know Pop. It takes a lot to get him to leave this house."

Trish yelled at someone. "Coming! Listen, gotta go. Helping with the rug rats here at the school. See ya later. Bye!"

Christie had barely told her goodbye, when the phone went dead. "Ugh, have to get this charged." She went back into the living area and surveyed her surroundings. The house would have fit right in with the tiny house movement. The living room with a door to a short hallway, the kitchen with a small dining area, two small bedrooms, and one bathroom. It's funny how different and smaller things became once time had gone by.

What had been Christie's old room now held an assortment of her mother's things that should have been given away long ago. She knew it would never happen while her father was still alive. Even after the many decades since her mother's passing away, it astounded her with the way it still affected her father. He'd moved on primarily for her sake but even though he'd been about Christie's current age when her mother had passed away, he'd never remarried.

His chair was empty. When she didn't find him in the house, or in the front area, she went back through to the kitchen and out the door. She called out from the back porch, "Pop?"

"Out here!" He waved at her as she watched him enter the barn. She knew better than to head out to the barn in her flip-flops, so she went back inside and scrounged in her suitcase until she found some boots. She pulled them on and strode out to the yard, the back screen door slapping closed behind her.

Entering the barn, it took a minute for her eyes to adjust to the dark interior. Then, she saw it. A small foal nuzzling its mother. "Oh, Pop. How adorable. When?"

"Done come on this spring. We weren't sure, though. Curtis had taken her in after the vet called, saying the horse had been abandoned.

People like that—"

Christie laid her hand on his arm. People were one thing, but her Pop couldn't abide anyone that would harm or neglect an animal. He stroked the mare.

"Poor neglected mama needed some extra care, didn't ya, girl?" He spoke softly to the horse. "I took her in when Curtis realized she was in the family way. He'd been fostering her in exchange for some vet care for his horses. I couldn't care for all his horses after the fire, but I can take care of her and her babe."

Christie grinned. "Well, glad you did, but Pop, how are you going to continue to take care of these horses? Not only are they a lot of work, but they're expensive on feed, shoeing, the vet bills..."

"Don't you go worrying your mind now, darling." He walked down to the next stall, where another mare approached the door.

"What's that tape on her neck?"

"Some new-fangled tape that's supposed to help with her neck strain. Kinsey—"

"Kinesiology tape?" Christie had heard about

the tape, but this was her first time seeing it on horses.

The nag nuzzled Pop, and he pulled a carrot from his pocket. "Here you go, old girl." He gave the horse the treat. "This here is old Curtis's horse. She got hurt a bit when she got spooked by the fire, so I'm just keeping her over here for a bit until he can figure out what to do. I couldn't handle the geldings, so they went to Moore's ranch."

"But—" Christie stroked the mare's muzzle.

"No butts. Ya gots to help your neighbors. That's what the Good Book says, and I'm doing it."

She raised her hands. "Sure." The foal trotted over to them on wobbly legs. Christie crouched down and let it come to her.

"Ah, she's already used to people and treats. There're some apples and carrots over in that bucket." Christie gave one to the foal, who quickly trotted back beside her mother. She pulled a cut apple from the bucket and, stretching her hand out flat, gave it to the mare. She stroked the horse between its ears.

"Hey, Pop, I'm meeting Trish over at Bum-doodlers. Want to join us?"

"Nah. I got my own plans."

"Okay."

"I wouldn't mind me a piece of pecan pie, though. How's about I stop by after I'm done?"

"That works. We're meeting at 1:30, if you can come. Will you have your truck with you? Why don't I drop you where you need to go?"

"I'll drive myself but meet you there."

"Okay." Christie kissed her father on the cheek and went back to the house. She pulled a maxi brown skirt and burnt orange and teal tank-top from her hanging bag. Grabbing two bar-rettes, she gathered her hair back off her face where she clipped them over her left ear. On her ears, she hung a pair of large copper hoops. Christie added a woven, russet, leather belt slung low on her hips and finished the outfit with some teal espadrilles. Pulling on her worn denim jacket, she slung her bag over her shoulder.

She came out of the bathroom as her father entered the kitchen. "Oh-ee. You're looking mighty pretty, darling. Watch out for them boys in town."

"Sure, Pop. I'll do that."

She walked out to her Jeep. She'd parked it under the old oak in the yard, so, luckily, the heat wasn't overbearing as she climbed inside. Starting the car, she backed out and headed down the dirt road with the AC blasting as high as it would go. She smiled at her father's words. Even in her forties, her father still thought of her as his little girl. Truth be told, she'd never been little, either. She'd worn a size ten-twelve in high school, and now she wore a fourteen on her good days but usually, a sixteen. Between her height of five-eleven and her muscles from helping patients up and down, she could carry extra weight better than most.

She took the back road to Boerne, enjoying the scenic route afforded on FM473 and the memories of simpler times hanging out at the old railroad bridge. Passing the historical bat house, she marveled at the thought of collecting bat guano for gunpowder. All she knew was that she was thankful for bats that kept the pesky mosquito population down.

Pulling into the Bumdoodlers parking lot, Christie drove around to park in the back, off to the side. The lot provided little shade, but she wanted to find a spot out of the way. Inside, she walked through to the front of the restaurant and found Trish staring at the pie display.

"Finally. I'm about ready to order all of those pies." She laughed and pulled Christie into a big hug. "Look at you. You always look so hot. No wonder the boys were always after you in school."

"I think it was more because I was the first to develop."

"See... hot." She hugged Christie again.

"Yep. That's me, all right. Hot. I need some iced tea."

"So happy to see you. How long has it been?"

"A while." Christie realized that it had been many years since she'd been home to visit. She'd need to change that and make more time to spend with her father now that he was getting on in years.

They went up to the counter, where Marie

Chambers waited, her coppery locks courtesy of the local salon, piled in a messy bun on top of her head. "Christie? Girl, give me a hug!" She came around the counter and hugged her. "Good to see you. How long are you going to be in town?"

"I'm not sure. Probably a couple of weeks."

"Well, I'm sure R.C. is glad you're home."

Christie nodded. People would call her father R.C. or Pop, but no one ever called him by his name, Rupert Constantine. The last person who had called him Rupert, who wasn't his mama, received a black eye for their troubles.

Marie went back around the wood partition. "What'll ya have?"

"I'll take a sweet tea..." Christie glanced over at the chalkboard hanging on the post.

"Is there any other kind?" Trish and Marie asked in unison.

"And the Brainstorm and a piece of pecan pie."

"Oh, sorry, sweetie. We're outta pecan. Everybody must be in the mood for it today. I've got a great coconut cream pie."

"Okay." Christie took the glass Marie handed her. She stepped to the side, where the large containers held tea, and filled the red plastic tumbler so Trish could complete her order for the Gobbler turkey sandwich. Christie handed Marie some cash but was shooed away by Trish. "My treat."

Stuffing the money back in her purse, Christie headed to the back area, where it was quieter. She sat down and waited for Trish to grab her drink.

Marie brought their food and they were chatting and laughing when a figure stepped up to their table. Kimberly stood before them with a full face of on-point makeup and platinum blond hair which tumbled down her back in curls. She'd accessorized her hair with large rhinestone clips that held her hair back off of her face. Christie hadn't spoken to Kimberly since high school.

"Well, I'd heard you were back in town. It's so good to see you. After all these years. I know you probably don't recognize me, now that I'm older and have put on weight. I try, but you know how it goes after you have kids." Her words came out sickly sweet, and a knot formed in Christie's stomach. It was just like Kimberly to play off something to fish for compliments. Even though Kimberly looked even thinner than she had in high school, Christie and Trish remained tight-lipped.

When she realized no compliments were forthcoming, Kimberly plopped down in a chair next to them. She stole a potato chip from Christie's plate, just like she used to do in high school. A strange feeling of deja vu hit Christie.

Kimberly wiped her hands with a napkin. "So what brings you to our neck of the woods? Visiting your dad? You know my mom and dad moved down to Mexico?" She barely took a breath before continuing. "They couldn't stand this heat. They don't get to see us as much now. But I guess that works for them. I have too many commitments here. I'm the board chair of..." She droned on and on, waving a huge, gaudy diamond on her left hand.

Finally, Trish interrupted. "I'd been asking Christie about her life since she left."

"Oh, well. Um, yes. I so want to hear about

your life, too." She smiled, but it never reached her eyes. A pained expression crossed her features, but she didn't get up to leave. Instead, she glanced at her phone screen, occasionally typing something on it.

Seriously rude. Christie answered simply, "Not much to tell. Went to school. Became a hospice nurse—"

"Oh, I couldn't do that. All those people dying. How sad." Kimberly picked up her phone again and typed.

Christie sighed. "You do know that you will die, right? Everyone dies. The job of a hospice nurse is extremely important."

"Oh, yes. I know, one time I—"

Trish cut Kimberly off. "Christie, tell us about that time when you got stuck in a blizzard with a murderer. I find the whole thing about what makes people kill so interesting."

"Oh, girls." Kimberly glanced at her phone. "So sorry. Have to run. Prior engagement. Let's get together. Kiss. Kiss." She stood and flounced out the backdoor as Marie arrived with their pie.

"That woman," Marie said under her breath.

Trish laughed. "Tell us how you really feel, Marie."

Marie pulled out a chair and sat down. "You know I'm not one to gossip..."

Christie smiled because gossipers always begin their stories with that disclaimer before they launch into gossip—the juicier the better.

"Of course not," Trish winked at Christie and turned back to Marie. "Now, spill."

"Well," Marie leaned in closer, and the two women followed suit, "I've heard she's been stepping out on Cole."

"Noooo." Trish put her hand on her chest.

"Yep. She thought he'd have his own real estate agency by now, but he's content working for the Websters."

Christie looked around for her phone. She must have left it in the Jeep. "Hey, ladies, I forgot my phone. I need it in case Pop calls." She wanted her phone, but also to escape the gossip. Her mother instilled in her at an early age that, if people will talk to you about others, they'll talk to others about you. According to her mom, gossip should have been one of the deadly seven sins, as it fits right in with some others like envy, malice, and pride. She took a quick bite of dill pickle and wiped her hands with a paper napkin. "I'll be back in a jiff."

The two women nodded but continued their conversation. Outside, it took a minute for Christie to adjust to the bright light. The heat hit her like a hot, wet blanket across her face. Over on the side, she noticed her father's truck. She started toward it, when angry voices startled her. They came from behind a large, white truck.

Wait, is that Hector's truck?

The voices were muted, but it was clearly an argument. It felt like slow motion as Christie swiveled to see her father move toward her, moving around behind the vehicle. The large truck backed up coming close to where her father walked toward her.

He must not see him. "Pop! Watch out!" Christie cried.

Pop moved backward but not quickly enough. The truck shot out of the parking lot, and as it did, the side panel of the truck pushed past Pop, sending him spinning. He fell and landed hard on his right shoulder. The truck took off from the lot.

"Help! Someone help!" Christie screamed as a couple ran over from their Chevy suburban. "Pop! Don't move. Are you hurt?"

"What do you think? I'm just in this heap on the ground for fun?" He winked at her, but a grimace quickly took its place. "Darling, I think I hurt myself."

Christie knelt in the dirt as she assessed him. "Where does it hurt, Pop?"

"My shoulder. Bad."

He had to have seriously injured himself if he would admit to his shoulder being hurt. People rushed out of the building, along with Trish and Marie. "What happened?"

"Some idiot in a truck sped out of here and wasn't watching where they were going. He barely missed hitting my father. If I wouldn't have been here, who knows—" She fought back angry tears.

Christie held onto her father, assessing his vitals as time slowed to a crawl. Finally, Christie could hear sirens. "Pop. Help is on the way. Don't you worry."

He grimaced and took shallow fast breaths.

"Over here!" People waved to the ambulance while others joined the crowd to see what was happening.

As they loaded her father onto the stretcher, he complained about having to go to the emergency room.

"Pop, I'll follow you there. Where are your keys for your truck?"

He tried to retrieve them from his pocket, but he winced and stopped short.

"What pocket, sir?" the female EMT asked.

After he pointed to his right hand pocket, he laid back on the stretcher. The woman tossed the keys to Christie.

"We'll be taking him to the Emergency Center for evaluation."

"Okay, I'll follow you there." She leaned over and rested her hand on his leg, "Pop, I'll be there soon. Love you."

"You don't need to..." A grunt of pain silenced him. "Love you, too."

The EMT shut the doors, and Christie watched as it left the parking lot.

Trish touched her arm, and Christie jumped. "Sorry. I didn't want to interrupt while you were talking to your dad. I can get Jess to take your Pop's truck home, so you don't have to worry about it."

"You don't need to do that. Plus, if you only knew how he is about others driving his truck..."

"Okay. Your Jeep then." Trish brushed her hair off her face.

"How did you know I had a Jeep?"

Trish shrugged. "Good guess."

Tears sprung to Christie's eyes.

"Ah, hon, you don't need to cry. Your dad will be fine."

Christie wiped her eyes. "Yes, I know. Thanks. I hate to impose on you all. What about his practice?"

"Jess can take the Jeep over with him, and I'll

follow him out to y'all's place and bring him home. No worries. Now, shoo."

They hugged, and Christie gave her the Jeep keys before heading to Pop's truck. Inside, she waited for the air conditioning to kick in and her adrenaline to calm down. She waved to Trish and headed toward the medical center. As she drove, anger built back up inside. Had it been Hector driving that truck? Had it been an accident, and he hadn't seen her father? Or had he meant to scare the old man and got too close? She couldn't imagine him trying to run him down on purpose. Who had the person driving the truck been arguing with? Maybe he had been so caught up in the argument, he didn't see her father walking toward the café. All she knew was that Webster Realty would hear from her. No way would Pop sell his property to them.

Over my dead body.

A shiver went up her spine. Christie chose to believe it was sweat interacting with the air conditioning and not a premonition.

Chapter Three

Christie sat in the doctor's office thumbing through an old magazine. Her father had broken his clavicle and while he had broken his humerus too, luckily, he wouldn't require surgery. Other than bruises on his side and legs, he'd fared pretty well for being mowed down by a large truck.

"I told you. You didn't have to come to the doctor with me." He grasped the sling on his arm.

"Pop, I want to hear how much physical therapy you will need. You cannot use that arm. So how do you expect to take care of yourself?"

"You have to get back to work. I don't want to be like those old folks who burden their kids."

Christie smiled. Even though her father was in his seventies, old was someone in their eighties or nineties. "I just want to make sure you're okay, that's all. Plus, I have taken very little of my leave, and they told me I could take as long as I want."

She didn't tell her father she'd given notice before they'd advised her to take a longer break and decide on her next steps. She hadn't known her break from work would include her father breaking his arm. Plus the idea that it could have been on purpose still crept into her thoughts. If she hadn't have been there, it could have been much worse. "Do you want me to fill out the form for you?"

"No. I already done it while you were parking the car. I could've walked. My legs ain't broke, you know."

"Pop, it's hotter than Hades out there."

"Hey, now. No need for cussing, missy." He shifted in his seat and rubbed the splint on his arm. "Itching like crazy."

A nurse appeared at the door and looked down at the chart, a hint of a smile on her lips. She spoke to the room, "Handsome."

R.C. struggled to get up from his chair. "That'll be me."

Other patients chuckled under their breath. Christie rolled her eyes behind her father. Leave it to him to write "handsome" under "what do you prefer to be called" on the form. She followed him as he shuffled toward the nurse.

"Mr. Handsome." The nurse held the door open for him.

"Darling, no need to be formal. You can just call me handsome." He moved past the young nurse, who waved Christie in with a wink.

When the doctor arrived, he introduced himself and pulled up the x-ray that had been taken in the emergency room. "Looks like you got the trifecta here—broken clavicle, scapula and humerus. As you can see, the humerus—that's your arm bone—has a break here. Not too bad, but it could have been a lot worse. I do see some early signs of osteoporosis, but nothing that would have caused this. The way you fell probably caused the breaks. Your collarbone broke when you tried to stop your fall. But you still landed hard enough to break your shoulder." He looked at the chart. "Says here it was a vehicle accident?"

"No. Some durn crazy driver hit me with their truck."

"Oh. That's terrible. Have you filed charges?"

Christie interjected. "We don't think they knew my father was there when they backed up and he was so close to it that the truck's large fender caused him to fall. He could have been in the driver's blind spot and with the windows up and music playing, the driver probably just wasn't aware of what happened." She didn't say anything about the fight that had occurred just before he sped out of the parking lot. "Anyway, I'm going over there today to speak with them. What does the prognosis look like?"

"We'll put him in a functional arm brace and keep him in the Figure Eight sling for about four weeks. During that time, we'll have him start PT."

Christie shifted in her seat. "I'm a nurse. I can help my father with this. What types of exercises are recommended? Pendulum? Others?"

"Yes. That would be good. I'll give you a prescription for pain Mr. Taylor, but only take them if you need them. They will make you drowsy, so you don't want to be driving." He pushed a pad with what looked like hieroglyphics on it toward them. Christie took it and put it in her purse. "Also, you can do heat packs or if you prefer, ice packs if that helps. Any questions?"

"Yes. How long do I have to wear this dadburn contraption?"

"Mr. Taylor, it depends on how fast your body heals and if you are consistent with the exercises your daughter will help you with on a daily basis. That said, we're probably talking somewhere in the neighborhood of six to eight weeks."

R.C. sat forward in his chair. "Six to eight weeks! I don't have time—"

"Mr. Taylor, you're a very lucky man. At your age, you could have broken a hip or required surgery. Give it some time to heal, then do the exercises, and we'll see you back in a few weeks. Then, we can decide on next steps, okay?"

"Thank you, doctor. I'll see that he does them." Christie rose and shook the doctor's hand.

The doctor stood and shook R.C.'s hand. "If you'll make an appointment with the nurse for, let's say, four weeks from now, then we can get a good idea of how you're progressing."

"Mr. Taylor." He patted him on his good arm. "We'll get you fixed up in no time."

They went out to the front desk, made the appointment, and returned to the lobby. As they walked through, the nurses all chimed in, "See you later, handsome."

He smiled and tipped his gray felt hat.

~~~

Christie stopped at H.E.B. to get Pop's prescription. She parked and left the Jeep running, since her father was now snoring away. As she left the pharmacy counter, she ran into Kimberly, who was pushing a basket full of groceries, her face down, her gaze glued once again on her phone.

"Hi, Kimberly."

She jumped. "Oh, Christie. You startled me." She put her hand to her chest and thrust her phone in her pocket. "So terrible about your dad. Is he okay?"

"Broke his shoulder, but with some physical therapy, he should be okay."
~~~

"Oh, that's a relief." She set her iced coffee drink into the holder on the full basket.

Christie looked at the items in the basket then back to Kimberly.

Kimberly hesitated. "Hmm, we're having a party to celebrate our anniversary. Twenty-five years." She hesitated. "Um, you could come."

"Thanks, but I need to stay with my dad."

Relief passed over Kimberly's face. "Well, you know you're more than welcome." She smiled.

"Kimberly, I know you'd left a few minutes before. Did you see who was driving a big white truck? I think it was one of the Webster's trucks with the decal on the door."

Kimberly hesitated again. "Nope, no. Can't say I did. I must have left before your dad was hit by the side of the truck. Will you be going home soon?"

Christie studied Kimberly. Why was she lying? She had to have been there to know that the truck hitting her father caused him to fall. Then, it hit her. Kimberly was the one having the argument with whoever was in that truck. Could it have been Hector? She realized she hadn't answered Kimberly, who was staring at her quizzically. "Sorry. So tired after yesterday."

"So, when are you going home?" Kimberly repeated her question.

"Home?"

"You know. Leaving?" Her sickly-sweet tone was one Christie was far too familiar with, having dealt with patients families who tried to con her by using the fake tone.

"This is my home."

"I know that, silly. I meant, back to where you came from."

Frustration bubbled up inside at the "where you came from," statement. Christie shot back. " I'm not sure when, or even if, I'll be leaving. Now, if you'll excuse me, my father, who was almost killed yesterday, is waiting on this medicine." She stormed off.

Whoa. Where had that come from? She had never been one to cause a scene, but something about Kimberly and the way she spoke to her had grated on her last nerve.

In the truck, she realized that the anger was actually toward whoever had been so negligent that they'd almost run over her father. As soon as she got him settled at home, she would pay Webster Realty a visit.

However, when she rounded the bend on the drive, she saw a white truck sitting in front of the house. As she pulled closer, a man got out of the truck.

No. It couldn't be. Not today.

It was Cole.

She parked under the tree, cracked the windows, and opened the door. She exited the Jeep and moved to help her father out of the vehicle, but Cole had already made it to the passenger side.

"Please let me help you." Cole opened the door and helped R.C. up to the porch. Christie silently followed. Cole eased open the front door and helped him into a chair next to the AC unit.

"I'm a mighty bit tired, sonny. No offense." Pop struggled to keep his eyes open.

"None taken, sir."

Christie poured a glass of water and handed her father a pill. "Take one of these, Pop. I'd rather we be proactive in managing the pain."

The old man took the pill and spoke to Cole. "You always were a good kid."

Cole grinned. "Thanks, Mr. Taylor."

"Mr. Taylor's my father. You can call me R.C. now you're all grown up like."

"Sir." Cole nodded.

"Cole, a word?" Christie cocked her head. "Outside."

They walked in silence.

"Was it you who nearly mowed my father down?"

Cole raised his hands in protest. "Do you really think so little of me that I would do something like that and not even stop?"

"How do you know they didn't stop?" She crossed her arms over her chest.

He leaned his back up against the tree. "Kimberly told me."

Oh, yes. Kimberly. She, who said she hadn't been there. But if she hadn't been arguing with

Cole, who had she been arguing with? Maybe she could get more information by not telling him that Kimberly had told her she'd left by then. "Yes, Kimberly had been visiting with me and Trish before the…" What was it… an accident? Or something else?

He took off his Stetson and ran his fingers over his eyebrows. She smiled. He'd had that quirky habit even back in high school. Her heart clenched.

"What are you doing out here, Cole?"

"Hector told me he came out to speak with your father, and R. C. pulled a shotgun on him."

Christie motioned over to a pair of chairs under a clump of large old oaks her parents had planted when they'd first married. Cole followed her. "You know my father. All bark and no bite. He wouldn't have done anything."

"Well, Emma seems to think—"

"And who's Emma?"

"The owner of Webster Realty." He crossed one leg over the other.

"Oh, yeah. I'd forgotten. Continue." She motioned with her hand.

"Anyway, she thinks Hector should file charges."

"What?" Christie shot up from her chair.

"Hear me out, okay?" He pulled a legal-size envelope from his pocket. "According to witnesses, they saw one of the Webster trucks leaving the scene. Now, we have lots of agents who have these trucks. As you can see, I have one, Hector does, the Websters do, and a few others. Whenever anyone closes on a major deal, the Websters get them a truck."

"That's a pretty nice gift."

"They still own them. Good tax write-offs, I guess."

He placed his hat back on his head. "Anyway, she's talked to Hector, and he's agreed to drop the charges against your father if he accepts this check and signs the enclosed document saying he won't pursue any further charges against the Webster organization."

"Are you kidding me? She's trying to buy us

off by saying they'll come after an old man if we don't take this?" She started pacing back and forth. "Who does she think she is? My father could have been killed if the truck had been any closer."

"Chrissy." His voice stopped her.

"Do. Not. Call me that. Only my best friends called me that."

"We used to be friends."

"The keywords there are 'used to.'"

Cole rubbed his stomach. "Can you hold on a minute?" He went over to the truck and opened the back passenger door. Inside, was an ice chest. He pulled out a bottle of a blue electrolyte concoction. "Want one?"

She shook her head and sat back down in the chair.

He took a big swig. "I've been fighting a horrible stomach bug, and it keeps hanging on. This heat doesn't seem to help it." He sat down next to her, moaning a bit as he clutched at his stomach. "Listen, take the check and talk to your father. All you know is that it was a white truck and maybe one of the Websters trucks. These are magnetic signs. They could make a case that someone took the sign and put it on their truck."

"Who would do that?"

"The point is, it could present reasonable doubt."

Cole took another swig of the drink and handed her the envelope. "Take the money."

"What happened to you, Cole? You used to be on the side of right and wrong."

"Well, you aren't exactly perfect either, now, are you?"

Christie rose from her chair. "What's that supposed to mean?"

He shook his head. "It doesn't matter now, anyway. It's all water under the bridge."

"Yes. It doesn't matter now," she replied as he got up and moved to the truck.

"Oh, and, congrats. Kimberly told me today that it is y'all's twenty-fifth wedding anniversary."

He stopped and turned around. They stared at one another.

"Take the money."

She watched as he drove off.

57

Chapter Four

The following morning, Christie was drinking cof-fee when her dad's landline phone rang. It tended to get better reception, so she rarely used her phone since being home. It had been nice to not be attached to the phone since being here, but she hadn't seen it in a while. She'd probably left it in the console in her Jeep, so she'd look for it later and make sure she charged it up.

"Hello?"

"Hey, Chica." It was Trish. "Wanta go out for a ride this morning?"

While the idea of getting out in the heat wasn't particularly inviting, riding the hundred-acre property would be nice. She knew there were cool spots with trees, and they could go down to the creek so the horses could drink.

"Sounds good, but we don't have any horses for riding."

Trish responded, "Oh, no worries. I've got two geldings which we rescued, and they are the sweetest boys. I'll bring them over in the trailer."

"Okay, how long do you think you'll be?" Christie shifted the phone to her other ear.

"Forty-five minutes or so."

"That's pretty quick, isn't it?"

"I knew you'd say yes. The tack is already loaded. All I have to do is load up the boys and head over."

Christie laughed. "You know me too well. I'll be ready." She ended the call and took a swig of coffee.

Pop set his cup on the table. "So you all are riding the property? How's about you check the fence line while you're at it?"

"We can, but I'm not sure we'll get to the entire perimeter. We're not planning on spending the entire day out."

"Wimps." Pop grinned.

Christie got up and washed her cup, hanging it on a hook over the sink. "Is there any place you want us to check?"

He nodded. "Yep. Check the fence along the Altgelt property."

"Any particular reason, Pop?"

"One of his cows got over here just before you arrived home. I planned on getting out to check it, but then," he raised his arm, then thought better of it and put it back down, "this happened."

"Okay, we'll check it out." She hated to bring it up but figured now was as good a time as any. "Pop, what did you decide about accepting the check? That is a lot of money." It had surprised Christie to see a check for $25,000 written out to R.C. Taylor. The note read, "gift for recovery." They'd covered their bases on that one. They could probably even write it off as a gift on their tax return. They had written nothing that would show culpability in the accident.

"The Websters are crazy if they think I'm taking their stinking money. Not one red cent. Look what they have done to others. They've increased the pressure on Curtis, too. I'm going over to see him in a bit."

"Pop, you can't drive. I'll take you over later if

you want to go."

He shifted in his seat. "I can drive. I've still got the use of this hand." He wiggled his fingers on his good arm.

"How 'bout I make you a deal? If you wait and let me drive you over, I'll make your favorite pecan pie?" Making a pie in the heat of summer wasn't appealing, but she knew nothing else would appease her father.

"Done." He raised his cup, and Christie poured him some more coffee.

"Do you need anything else while I'm out with Trish?"

He shook his head. "You have fun."

Christie rummaged through her suitcase to get a long sleeve shirt she could wear over the tank top. She found an old baseball cap and tied a bandana around her neck. She was just pulling on her boots when she heard a truck pull up.

"That can't be Trish yet." Christie went over to the door.

Oh, no. A Webster vehicle.

A petite woman with a mountain of bleached

blond hair piled on top of her head stepped down onto the automatic step from the truck.

Good grief. It's like Sweden around here with all the blondes.

She waved at Christie who moved out onto the porch.

"Hi-ya," she trilled. She wore three-inch stilettos with red soles, a colorful peplum top, and white pants with decorative gold buttons up the sides. As she approached the porch, the first thought that came to Christie was "firecracker."

The woman reached the porch steps and thrust out her hand. "Hello. I'm Emma Webster. I just came by to see how y'all are doing and see if I could pick up that letter." She smiled, revealing bright, white, straight teeth. Veneers. They were almost as shiny as the huge round diamonds in her ears. Christie noted that she also had an enormous gem on her left hand.

"I'm sorry, but it seems you've come out here for nothing. My father will not accept your check."

The woman's face crumpled but her eyes stayed hidden behind her Chanel sunglasses.

Am I getting ready to see an adult have a toddler tantrum?

The woman quickly composed herself and propped the sunglasses up on her head like a tiara. She smiled up at Christie. "Now, y'all take as much time as y'all need. No hurry. We just want what's best for your father."

I'll bet you do.

Christie replied, "Well, it's good you came out here because my father also wants to let you know that he is not, nor will he ever, sell this property."

The woman's eyes flashed with irritation, but she kept a smile on her painted pink lips. "Of course. No need to think about that right now. I wanted to let you know that we're in negotiations with Curtis Altgelt to sell his property. After his barn fire, he's giving our offer more consideration."

That came as a shock, but Christie remained silent.

"We will make him and his heirs very wealthy people." Her implied note about heirs was so blatant, Christie almost wanted to laugh out loud.

"Well, good for them." Christie could play this game, too. She'd had to deal with enough greedy family members, who cared nothing for the person in her care. Vultures, she'd called them. Emma also fit that bill.

"I would just hate to see y'all not get a good asking price for this place. Some places have been found to have contamination in the soil or water, and the owners practically have to give it away. Or eminent domain for roads and such. It's just so... sad."

Christie kept her cool. "Well, as we have no intention of selling or giving anything away, we'll be just fine."

The woman exhaled, pushed her sunglasses onto her nose, and gingerly made her way down from the porch. She started the vehicle remotely and turned back to Christie.

"Oh, one last thing. It appalled me to hear that your father threatened Hector with a shotgun. Waving a gun around could be mistaken as mental instability. I hope he's not suffering from the first signs of dementia or other issues. I've begged Hector not to press charges, but," she shrugged her shoulders, "there's not much I can do."

Just then, the screen door shot open. "I'll show you who's crazy! This is my property, and you're trespassing. You better leave now." Pop pulled a pistol from the back of his pants.

Emma squawked like a chicken being chased for dinner. She ran—as much as one can run in stilettos—to her truck and climbed up into the cab. She reversed quickly, and gravel sprayed from her tires as she backed up, barely missing Trish's truck and horse trailer coming down the road.

"Pop! Give me that. Are you trying to get arrested?"

"Naw. Just having some fun. This pistol belonged to my great-grandfather. It's not loaded, and it hasn't been fired in generations."

"They don't know that."

"Good. Then they should get the hint to stay off my property." He took the gun and went back inside.

Trish stood next to her truck door and pointed at the departing vehicle. "Am I mistaken or was that Miss Snooty Pants Webster?"

Christie laughed. "I guess that's as good a name as any."

"I gotta tell you that woman is strange, but it makes sense." Trish went to the rear of the horse trailer and opened the gate.

"What makes you say that?"

"Have you met her husband, Tyler, yet?" She backed a handsome gelding out of the trailer and handed the reins to Christie.

"No, can't say I have."

Trish went back into the trailer. "There's just something about him, that's all." She backed another horse out of the trailer.

Christie patted the American Paint's muzzle. "You're a handsome fella."

Trish swung the other horse around by the leads. "That's Champ, and this here good fella is Scout. We bought both of them from a ranch about a year ago. "Which one do you think you want to ride?"

Champ nuzzled Christie. "I think we have a winner." Trish had already saddled the pair, so Christie mounted Champ and took a few turns around the yard. She leaned down and stroked his neck.

"Oh, I forgot to grab drinks and snacks."

Trish patted the saddlebags she'd added to the back of Scout. "Got some right here. You ready?"

Christie nodded, and they walked the horses until they were away from the homestead. They picked up the pace, and once they hit a large patch of meadowland, Christie took Champ into a trot before squeezing her legs to get him to go into a canter. The ride was enjoyable and invigorating, and as the horses slowed back into a walk, they headed toward the fence line between the properties. Everything looked good, until they came to a section where the fence lay crooked with a large gap.

"What in the?" Christie dismounted, and Trish followed suit. Trish's quarter horse, Scout, lowered his head down and picked at a small patch of grass.

Christie bent down. "Look. Someone cut these wires. I know Curtis wouldn't have done that. I need to tell him and Pop about this. I don't have the tools, so I'll have to come back and fix it."

Trish wiped sweat from her face with a red bandana. "It's getting pretty hot, anyway. How about we head down and follow along the creek bed? We can let the horses drink and take a break."

"Sounds good to me." Christie swung herself back up on Champ and Trish followed.

They made their way over to the creek. After they let the horses drink and ate some snacks Trish had brought, they walked alongside the horses.

"Once we get up here, we can take the service road and—"

Trish squinted and pointed. "What's that?"

Christie looked ahead. A large white truck. Had Emma come down here after she'd left them? But that had been hours ago. A man in a white shirt staggered from the truck. He appeared to be moving with some difficulty.

"Come on." They got back up on the horses and trotted to the truck.

It was Hector.

Christie swung down from Champ and ran over to the man. "Hector, are you okay?"

"Don't feel so good." He vomited a blue liquid.

Trish had followed and held the reins of the horses. She blanched. "Ew. Gross."

"I've seen everything there is to see in my line of work. That's nothing." She crooked his arm over her shoulder and put her arm around his waist. "Come on, Hector. Let's get you into the shade."

He doubled over. "My stomach."

Christie noticed the lack of sweat on his brow. "Trish, I think he may have heat stroke. Let's get him something to drink."

Trish ran over to his truck and grabbed an electrolyte drink in the console. She held it up. "What about this? It's cold. I see he has an ice chest, so he must have gotten it from there." She handed it to Christie who took it but set it down on the ground.

"No, that's the worst thing you can drink when you're hot. You need cool or room temperature water. Grab some from your bags."

Trish ran over to Scout.

"Oh, no! He's losing consciousness. Trish, Call 911!"

Trish pulled out her phone. She cried out, "There's no signal!"

"Hurry! Ride to the house. Get help. I'll stay with him," Christie yelled.

Even as Trish took off with Scout at a full gallop, Christie knew it was a fool's errand. She checked Hector's pulse. His heart rate was elevated. She opened the neck of his shirt and poured water onto the bandana she'd brought with her. She wiped his head and neck, but his breathing grew more labored.

Trish, hurry. He doesn't have long.

Christie moved over so she could elevate his feet onto her legs. Her mind raced while time slowed. Why was Hector on their property and why had he come here? Had he meant to hit Pop, or had it truly been an accident? Cole had complained of a stomachache and now, Hector. Had they both gotten food poisoning from the same place? Or was this heat-related?

She spoke soothing words as she had done on many previous occasions when no family or friends were present. And Christine Taylor was once again the last person who heard a person's final breath.

Chapter Five

Trish had driven back with Pop in the truck. Christie wiped her eyes and bit her lip to quell the strong emotions washing over her.

When the truck stopped, her father launched himself out of the truck, spewing anger, "How is that no-good..."

"Pop, not now. He's dead." She stood up, wishing she had some way to cover Hector.

"What?" He took a step back and his jaw dropped open. Staggering, he caught himself by reaching over to the truck's hood. Shaking his head, he whispered, "I always liked that kid. Even if he did work for that woman."

Christie hurried over to his side and put her arm around her father. "I know. I did, too." She turned to Trish. "Is the ambulance on the way?"

Trish had made her way around the truck and stood beside them.

"Pop, there's nothing you can do here. Go home, and I'll be up in a while. Trish, can you take him back?"

He shrugged away from her. "No. I'll walk."

"But, Pop—"

"There's nothing wrong with my legs." He shooed her hand away and stumbled forward. As she watched, he turned around and walked over to Christie. "You did what you could." He leaned over and kissed her on the forehead.

Christie struggled to hold back the tears. "Thanks, Pop." She watched him walk back up the dirt track as she closed Hector's truck door.

Trish turned toward Christie. "Hector was such a nice guy. It's so sad. What could have happened?"

"I don't know. Did he have any health issues that you know of?" Christie's mind whirled wondering about Hector's presence on their property.

Trish sniffed. "I don't think so, but I'm not sure how I would know that. What do you think he was doing out here?"

"I'm wondering that, too. Though the service

road is used by the city sometimes, you rarely find people coming out here on a whim."

"Remember when we all used to meet down here when we were kids?"

The change of conversation surprised Christie. A man had just died. She was surprised at how callous Trish was treating the incident. Yes, there had been memories from the past, but they were now marred again by the death of Hector Garcia. "Yes, I do." She replied tersely.

She'd never told Trish about the time she'd waited and waited for Cole at this spot, but he'd never come. And how he'd acted like nothing had changed the next day. Even worse, he'd humiliated her by smiling in the lunchroom as if nothing had happened. After that, she had wanted nothing to do with Cole. It was as if Kimberly had been waiting for that moment. Cole, now the Cougars star quarterback, was a prime catch. His dad had money, and he drove the best truck in the senior class. When Kimberly snagged the head cheerleader position, it wasn't long before the two became a pair. Class favorites, prom king and queen, the list of their achievements went on. When Christie heard the news that the pair were engaged, she was happy to leave town and never look back.

But time had a way of pulling her back to the past, and she had loved and missed the old homestead. Now another, more serious, tragedy had happened.

"Earth to Christie." Trish waved her hand in front of Christie's face.

"Sorry. In my own world." She looked up to see the sheriff's cruiser and an ambulance coming down the old service road. She waved at them. They turned and navigated down toward the creek. A tall, deeply tanned man stepped out from his patrol vehicle.

"Hug?"

"Christie! Well, I'll be." The Sheriff's face broke out in a big grin.

She remembered the boy who had been a few years behind her in high school. His baby sister, Suzanne, could never pronounce his name, Hugh, so he'd become "Hug" to everyone.

He walked over to her and wrapped her in his big, beefy arms.

"Sheriff Clauson now, huh?"

"Yep. So, fill me in on what happened here."

Christie sensed his changed demeanor as he moved back into his professional role. The Sheriff asked a few things but said they could go back to the house and he'd go up there and speak with them. Trish had somehow gotten Champ back up to the house, so they climbed into her father's old pickup. They rode in silence back to the house.

Even though Christie had seen many deaths in her time, something troubled her spirit about Hector's death. She turned to Trish. "I have to find out if Hector had health issues. What was he doing out here by himself? Sure, heat stroke happens but something doesn't feel right."

"I could see if Shana May could let you into his house."

"What do you mean?" Christie turned off the truck after parking it next to her Jeep.

"She does housecleaning, and I'm fairly sure she does Hector's house. I can ask."

Christie pushed her hair back off her face. "I don't know. I'm not sure that would be right."

"Look, he's dead."

"Trish!" Her lack of empathy stunned Christie.

"Okay, sorry. But we could get into his house if we make her something—like a pie. Then, we could just say we knew she'd be there." She grinned.

"You are a piece of work, you know?"

Trish laughed. "You have no idea. But you still like me."

"Yes, I do." She lowered her head and grinned. "Even if you are crazy."

They heard a vehicle coming up the road.

Trish shielded her eyes with her hand. "Oh, geez. Here comes trouble."

"Look again. Double trouble." Christie crossed her arms and waited.

The truck screeched to a halt, and Emma Webster exited the truck. The other door opened, and Kimberly slid out of her side, steadying herself on her heels.

"Is it true? I just got a call. What happened?" Emma spat at them.

"Whoa, there. Settle down." Christie held up her hands to fight off the vitriol.

"Don't tell her to settle down. Hector comes here, and your dad takes a shot at him. Now he's found dead on *your* property."

"Now wait a minute," Trish blustered until Christie spoke.

"First, my father did not take a shot at Hector—"

"Darn tooting." A gravelly voice spoke up from behind them on the porch.

Oh, great. The last thing I need is for Pop to get involved.

"Pop, I was explaining—"

"There's no need to explain anything to those two trollops."

Kimberly gasped.

"Wow, this reminds me of old times." Trish laughed. "You gonna run and tell your daddy, Kimberly?"

"You little…" Kimberly moved forward.

A male voice commanded, "Stop right there, Ms. Whitaker."

They turned to see Sheriff Clauson. He must have parked down by the old oak and walked the last bit up to the house.

Kimberly turned and pointed at Pop. "I want you to arrest him!"

"What?" Everyone echoed.

"He threatened Hector, and when Hector narrowly avoided him in the parking lot, well…"

"He didn't 'narrowly avoid' him. He almost killed my father."

"So, there you go, you both have motive." Emma Webster spoke up.

"Are you freaking kidding me?" Christie bristled and took a step toward Emma. "Now you're saying I killed Hector? And what, pray tell, would be my reason?"

"Revenge," Emma Webster replied.

Christie laughed. "Revenge? For what?"

"For almost hitting your dad. Then you wouldn't have to take care of him," Kimberly joined in.

Trish stepped forward. "What is this? Are you all on drugs? Christie's a nurse. No way would she hurt anyone. Or Mr. Taylor, for that matter. I'm fixin' to knock out some of those fake pearly whites if you don't apologize right now."

"See!" Kimberly pointed at Trish. "She threatened me! I want her arrested, too."

The sheriff walked closer to the group, and Christie watched as her father moved off the porch.

"Now, Hug, I've known ya since you were knee high to a grasshopper. No way would I or my Chrissy cause harm to anyone. You and everyone else here—even this girly—knows that's the truth of it. Hector came over and I'd been cleaning my shotgun. It wasn't even loaded. I keep telling this woman that I ain't selling this place, but she keeps sending those vultures over here. It's trespassing, plain and simple. As for poor Hector, no telling why he was on my property."

Emma answered. "Well, that's easy. He called me saying to meet him here. That he thought you all were planning on accepting our 'gift' or possibly wanted to talk about selling the property."

The Sheriff said, "We have his phone, and we'll see if the phone records agree with that."

"I never called Hector," Pop told Christie.

The Sheriff spoke into his walkie-talkie. "Deputy Roland, bring me Hector's phone."

He stuffed his thumbs into his gear belt as everyone glared at each other, but they all remained silent.

Roland arrived shortly and brought the phone over to the Sheriff. Clauson pulled on latex gloves and took the phone from the bag. "Unfortunately, it has a password on it. But—"

Kimberly said, "I think it's something like a G."

"You would know, since you've been having an affair with him." Trish thrust her chin out.

"How dare you!" Kimberly responded.

"What! Is this true?" Emma turned to Kimberly.

The Sheriff silenced them. "One call is to you, Emma. There's another call to Cole. And one text to an unknown number."

Emma spoke. "It could be from one of our clients. Read me the number, and I can let you know."

The Sheriff didn't have to finish all the numbers for Christie to know it was her phone number.

"Ring any bells?" the Sheriff asked.

"It's mine." Christie sighed.

"So, you texted Hector?"

"No."

"The evidence," he held the screen up for her to see, " says you did."

"I didn't. I'm telling you. What does it say?"

"Meet me at the old spot by the creek."

Christie gulped, but said nothing.

Sheriff Clauson asked, "Where's your phone now?"

"Um, in my Jeep, I think."

"Deputy, please go with Ms. Taylor and retrieve her phone."

Ms. Taylor now. Him not calling her by her

first name didn't bode well. Christie and the deputy walked over to the Jeep. She started to open the console when the deputy stopped her. He put on gloves and opened it.

The deputy did a search in the console before yelling out, "No phone, Sheriff."

"But it has to be there. I hadn't taken it out because I was bringing some things in from the store." She went to open the other door, but the deputy stopped her. She grunted in frustration. "Fine. Look under the seat. Maybe it fell under there."

The deputy searched inside, but the phone was not in the car.

"When was the last time you saw your phone, Christie?"

"As I said, I went into town for some supplies, then came back out here. I sometimes leave it in the car."

The sheriff handed the plastic bag with Hector's phone back to the deputy.

"And no one has had access to it during that time?"

"No..." She hesitated.

"Is there something you want to say?" Sheriff Clauson motioned for her to continue.

Christie's thoughts raced. Cole had been waiting for them, and they had taken Pop's truck to go to the doctor and get feed for the horses. Her mind raced. But why would Cole text Hector from her phone? What would he have to gain?

Oh, no. If Hector and Kimberly were having an affair, did Cole kill him?

She looked up. "Sheriff, I'm not feeling well. I'm still getting used to this Texas heat and humidity again. Can we go inside where it's cooler?"

"I think we have what we need for now. Just stay in town where I can reach you." He shook Christie's father's hand. "R.C."

"That's it? You're not going to arrest them or something?" Kimberly moaned.

"On what charge?"

Kimberly thought for a moment. "Well, um..."

Pop said, "I agree. Arrest them two." He pointed at the two women.

"What for?" Emma spoke.

"For trespassing on my property." He took the check out of his pocket, tore it into little pieces, and threw it up in the air. "And you can take this, too. Now git before I sic my dogs on ya."

"Sheriff!" Emma cried out. "You can't arrest me. I've done nothing wrong."

"This is his property. Unless you have permission to be here, I suggest you leave. Now."

The women headed back to the truck.

"This isn't the last you'll hear from me," Emma spat at them.

"Oh, goody." Christie waved.

After the Sheriff left, she looked at her father and Trish.

He pointed to the house. "Come inside, girl. I know you got something you want to share with us."

Chapter Six

When the group had settled in front of the air conditioning, Pop spoke. "Get it off your chest, Christie. I can see the wheels turning in your mind."

"Remember when we went out to eat? I didn't have my phone with me, so I went out to get it. I heard Hector arguing with someone. Now I think it was Kimberly."

"Could be." Trish pulled off her boots, propped her feet up on the sofa close to Christie, and took a sip of her iced tea.

Christie reached over and unconsciously began massaging Trish's foot. "Oh, my gosh. That's amazing. Do this one, too!"

"I'm so used to doing this for patients, I guess it's just a subconscious habit to start rubbing feet."

"I hope I'm not dying anytime soon." Trish rapped her knuckles on the worn oak table, "but

I'll take it a foot massage any day." Christie continued the massage as Trish let out a sigh of relief.

"Anyway, then he peeled out of there, and that's when you got hurt, Pop."

He rubbed his arm. "Yes, don't remind me. Dang kids and their fast cars."

Christie and Trish glanced at each other and grinned.

"Pop, Hector was our age. He was in his forties."

"Your point?"

"Um. Nothing."

A horn honked outside. "That'll be Jess. As much as I hate to leave while you're massaging my tootsies, I gotta go."

"Oh, geez. I didn't even notice your vehicle and horse trailer gone. I should have helped you with them."

Trish came around and hugged Christie. "You were a bit busy trying to save a man's life."

"I only wish I would have helped him." She shook her head and sighed. "I could tell he was close to death when we found him."

"Poor Hector. Not sure what happened there," Trish replied.

The horn honked again.

"That kid." She yelled out the door, "Hold yer horses. I'll be there in a minute." She turned to face Pop and Christie. "Ugh, teenagers. Gotta love'em, but you can't kill 'em." She wiggled her eyebrows.

"You still up for...you know, Christie? Tomorrow morning sometime?"

Pop sat back in his chair. "What are you two young-uns up to?"

"Nothing," they said in unison.

"Yep. That always means something."

"Pop, I told Trish I would make you a pecan pie tonight when the weather cools off, and she wanted me to make one for her, too."

"Now, don't go fibbing. I know when you two are planning something you don't want me to know."

"You're too smart for us, Pop." Trish kissed him on the cheek.

"And don't you forget it." He smiled.

Christie walked Trish to her truck, where Jess had moved over to the passenger side.

Trish walked toward the truck. The window was rolled down. "Say hello, Jess."

"Hello, Ms. Taylor." He slumped in his seat.

Trish turned back to Christie. "What time tomorrow?"

"Hmmm, let me call you. Oh, wait…" Christie thought for a moment.

My phone. Where is it? And who has it?

Even though Christie loved Trish like a sister, the idea of sharing the thought that Cole may have taken her phone was unthinkable. "I guess I'll be buying a new one tomorrow. Maybe one from this era. Until then, just call Pop's landline."

"Okay. Will do." Trish grinned and swung herself up into the driver's seat.

Christie waved as the pair drove off. Then, she grabbed her hat and sunglasses and walked down to the overlook. A tow truck was attaching Hector's vehicle. She rubbed her arms. What had happened to Hector?

She kicked at a clod of dirt. Why take her

phone and why text Hector to meet her?

"Oh no." If Hector died on their property right after he'd caused injury to Pop, that meant someone was trying to point the finger at her if his death wasn't natural.

So much for coming back to a simpler life. Death hadn't stayed behind but had followed her home.

~~~

As the sun set, Christie pulled ingredients to start work on the pecan pie. Normally, she made the pie crust from scratch, but she'd cheated and bought one from the store. When she'd brought it home, she'd gotten "the look" from her father and stashed it back in the freezer. Maybe she'd use it to make a quiche. Christie set to work making the piecrust. There was one key ingredient to her father's piecrust, and that was vegetable shortening. Her mother had wanted a large pantry space for all her canned goods and items that wouldn't do well in the Texas heat, so her father had built a cellar for her. Christie opened the door that led
~~~

down wooden stairs to the storage space, clicked on the light and made her way down into the cool room. She found the big blue tub and stuck it under her arm to carry upstairs.

Christie's mind went back to her childhood when the three of them would eat dinner in the small room during the hottest summer nights. Surrounded by canned goods from the harvest, the bounty offered comfort and security at the same time. Often, her folks would trade with others, in case a crop didn't produce enough for the year. Neighbors always helped neighbors. Times had sure changed in the years since the world had become so encapsulated behind computer screens and locked doors.

She worked her way down the rows to a batch of canned peaches. Eating a peach out of a jar was like taking a bite of summer. Pickled beets, onions, okra, and eggs were often in abundance. Onions hung from the ceiling in old stockings, and cases filled with sand would hold carrots and other root vegetables when they were ready for harvest. Large containers of beans, rice, flour, sugar, and cornmeal, among other staples, took up one wall. The bounty within the room meant that, no matter the state of the economy, they always ate—and ate well.

Christie remembered harvest time and all the work involved in preserving the food. She'd hated spending days peeling peaches or snapping peas. Now, she missed that time of laughter and conversations with the end result being a collection of jars full of nature's bounty.

The kitchen in the main house had been so small, Pop had built a larger kitchen that could expand in the summer onto a covered patio area where tables sat for preparation and cooling off of the jars. The sound of jar lids popping as they cooled had always brought smiles to faces.

Christie would prep the pie ingredients there, then assemble and cook them in the convection ovens in the outdoor kitchen. That way, it wouldn't heat the house, which was already struggling to remain cool with the living room window unit.

One year, her father sold off a prized bull to

pay for the commercial oven as a Christmas gift for her mother. She had loved it and used it for canning, along with baking pies and cakes for new moms, invalids, and others in need. Then, the cancer had struck. In a few short months, her mother went from a vibrant woman to a shadow of her former self.

Christie struggled to hold back tears that formed from remembering that difficult time. Losing a mother before blossoming into a young woman had forced her to grow up fast. Maybe it had even changed her and made her the independent woman she'd become. She still struggled with leaning on others for support. Her mother's death had devastated them all, but her father had suffered in silence. Always by his wife's side, he refused to leave until a hospice nurse had told him that she would ensure he was there if needed. As Christie saw the care the nurse gave to her patient, she'd decided the medical field was what she wanted as her career path. Everyone had always said she should become a therapist due to her listening skills. In some ways, that had come true as patients and family members trusted her with their long-held hopes, dreams, secrets and re-grets.

So many years later and the memory felt like it had happened yesterday. Christie gathered other ingredients in a big aluminum bucket and headed out back.

~~~

Pop Taylor's Texas Pecan Pie Recipe

First Step: Collect Your Ingredients

- 1 piecrust
- 1 cup sugar
- ½ cup dark corn syrup
- ½ cup light corn syrup
- 1 teaspoon vanilla extract
- 4 tablespoons butter (plus extra for brushing crust if desired)
- 1/8 teaspoon (pinch) salt
- 3 farm-fresh cage-free eggs (slightly beaten)
- 1 heaping cup chopped pecans (cut full pecans crosswise)
~~~

- Optional: Dark chocolate, melted (70+ percent) 2-3 squares

Second Step: Prepare Your Oven

Heat oven to 350 degrees (176.6 C)

Third Step: Gather Your Tools

- Baking pie pan (if not using store bought piecrust that included a pan)
- Measuring cups
- Measuring spoons
- Mixing bowls
- Spatula
- Knife
- Pastry brush (optional)
- Piecrust protector shield (optional)

Fourth Step: Assemble Your Ingredients

Mix sugar, syrup, salt, vanilla and butter.

Slightly beat eggs to break yolks and incorporate.

Add slightly beaten eggs to mixture and fold together.

Optional Step: Brush melted chocolate lightly over piecrust with pastry brush before filling

(Christie's version)

Place cut pecans into an unbaked pie shell.

Pour the filling over pecans.

Set filled pie pan on middle rack in oven.

Optional: Put piecrust protector shield on piecrust.

Fifth Step: Bake Your Pie

Bake at 350 degrees for 10 to 15 minutes (check your oven temp)

Then reduce heat to 325 degrees for 40 to 45 minutes.

Optional: If using piecrust protector shield, remove for first or last 15 minutes.

Optional: Last five-ten minutes brush piecrust with melted butter or egg wash.

Sixth Step: Check Your Pie

Test to see if the pie is done by lightly "shaking" the pie pan. The middle should have some jiggle to it but have a solid consistency, not watery. Conversely, insert a knife can be inserted in the middle of the pie and should come out clean. If done, remove from oven.

Seventh Step: Cool the Pie

Place the pie on a cookie cooling rack or other stand so that the bottom of the pie has circulation under it. Let the pie cool completely before cutting.

Eighth Step: Eat the Pie!

Notes:

Coating the piecrust can provide an added flavor but can also help with soggy piecrust bottoms.

Cut pecans make the pie easier to cut and you get pecans in every bite. The cut halves will surface at the top of the pie just like regular pecans.

In place of vanilla extract, brandy or whisky can be substituted.

According to safety standards, pecan pie should be placed (and kept) in the refrigerator within two hours.

~~~

The outdoor kitchen—as they called it—had been
~~~

closed for a long time. For a while the church ladies had used the kitchen when canning but over the years, it had been used less and less as people modernized their own homes. The space got some use when Christie came home during Thanksgiving and Christmas but that had dwindled in the last few years as work had taken over much of her life.

While enclosed from the elements, it had taken Christie a few days of elbow grease to get rid of all the spiders that had sought its shelter. Now, it shone and was ready for use once again.

Christie ambled out to the building, a large box of supplies in hand. She opened the screen door into the main front room, which was little more than a screened-in porch with shutters all around it for closing it up when not in use. She unlatched the sliding door that separated the appliance area from the outdoor space and flipped on the light switch. The lights illuminated the space while Christie rolled the stainless-steel island out from the cabinet area.

Christie set ceramic mixing bowls that she

would need for making the pie filling on the counters. The refrigerator was old but still useable and cold. Now, it mainly held watermelon and other things that couldn't fit in the smaller indoor fridge. She pulled the piecrust dough she'd made earlier from its interior. An old cassette-tape radio from the eighties stood on top of the fridge, and she turned it on. A nasally twang and a melody of fiddles and mandolin filled the air. Real country music—that's what Pop called it—crackled through the small speakers. She gathered the ingredients and set to work, humming along to older tunes she recalled from her youth. Christie made quick work of filling the pies after adding in chopped pecans like Pop preferred. As far as she knew, her mother had started chopping the pecans after Pop had complained about having pecans in one bite but not the next one. Ever since then, they'd kept preparing pecan pie that way.

The squeak of a screen door brought her out of her reverie. She looked up to see Pop standing in the door. "Supper's ready."

"Perfect timing, Pop. I was just finishing." She

completed loading all the tools back into the box and eyed the various pies cooling on the counters.

He cocked his head, listening for a moment. "I think they're playing our song, darling. Come on." He took her hand, and they two-stepped around the tiny space. A fleeting memory of watching her mother and father dance around the area came to her mind. She stifled a sob and rubbed at the tears on her cheeks.

"I miss her, too, darling." He squeezed her hand. "We can get that box later. Let's eat." He'd prepared black-eyed peas with roasted ham, collard greens, and cheesy grits. A plate sat on the table with a tea towel over it.

She smiled. "Oh, please tell me that's what I think it is."

"Yep. You're favorite. Fried green 'maters. Ain't nothing in this world..." he sang the familiar tune she'd heard so many times growing up.

"Pop, this is wonderful." Plates and silverware were already set at their places and in the middle a mason jar held a display of sunflowers and other wildflowers. They filled their plates with the home-cooked spread.

"Um. Hm," he muttered through a mouth full of buttered cornbread. He wiped his mouth. "Now, I want the truth from you, girl, and I ain't stopping 'til I hear it."

There was no use trying to keep something from her father. It was like he had a sixth sense about these things. She shared about the text to Hector coming from her phone and her suspicions about Cole taking her phone.

"That's something. I just don't see that boy doing something he shouldn't. Nope. Just can't see it. He's a good kid. I don't understand about your phone though."

"It's simple, Pop. If it looks like one of us lured Hector out here and then he dies—"

"Like to say one of us was to blame for his death?" Pop shook his head. "I don't see why someone would do that. Nope, not Cole. I won't believe it."

He took a swallow of cold buttermilk. "But that wife of his...never did like her. Whenever all y'all girls were together, I'd hear Ma say to herself, 'she's a bad' un.' You know your ma, bless her soul, always could read people like that."

"Yes, I'm not a fan of Kimberly, either, but if she *was* having an affair with Hector, I can't see why she'd want to kill him. What would she gain by that?"

Pop began to speak but instead speared a crispy tomato with his fork. "Maybe Hector was going to tell Cole."

"That's a possibility. But that would have consequences for him, too. They worked together. I can't see Emma letting both of them stay on after that announcement."

"*If* Hector was going to stay there." Pa cut a piece of ham and popped it in his mouth.

Christie laid down her fork. "Pop, you know something you're not telling me."

"All I'm saying is that maybe Hector decided he wanted to steer his life a different direction. In fact, he may have even been thinking about a new career."

"Pop, you're holding something back. What is it?"

"A few months ago Hector visited me. He hated how the Websters were so pushy about getting the Altgelt property and this property. He said it obsessed them. He was frustrated, and he told me that he wouldn't put it past them to have something to do with Curtis's barn fire."

"Really? He told you that?"

"To my face. He did." He picked up another fried green tomato.

"Wow. That changes everything. If Hector had information the Websters were involved in the fire, that could have potentially destroyed their business and sent them to jail."

He looked at Christie. "And give them a mighty good reason for Hector to be silenced."

Christie wiped her mouth with a napkin. "This is getting crazier and crazier. Pop, what're we going to do?"

He pointed his fork at her. "*We* ain't gonna do nothing. Stay out of it. Hug can handle it."

"But someone has my phone and used it to text Hector. That will not go away."

He nodded. "That is something. But we got to

give it time."

"Pop, I don't like you being out here by your-self. If the Websters tried to burn down the barn, who's to say they won't try something here?" She took a drink of tea. "Maybe they're the ones who cut the fence line."

"What?"

"Oh, in all the commotion, I forgot to tell you. Way out past that grove of cedar and mesquite, someone cut the fence line. That's probably how Curtis's heifer got over here."

"Were there tire tracks?"

"I didn't notice any, but I didn't get off the horse and look. There were some other tracks, but I figure they were from animals crossing there. Deer trails, maybe."

"Tomorrow, I've got to go talk to Curtis."

Christie picked up the dishes and put them over at the sink. "Pop, let me go with you. I have to go with Trish in the morning, but I can take you over in the afternoon after your exercises."

He sighed. "I hate those exercises. They hurt."

"You may hate them, but you'll hate not having the full use of your arm if you don't do them. You never let me know it was hurting. We'll go easier. Don't overdo it, okay?"

"Fine. Now you go on and get them pies inside. I can manage here."

"You did pretty well on this meal for someone with only one hand."

"Actually," he winked, "the church ladies brought this over. I think they forgot you're here. All I did was fry up the 'maters."

"If that's the case, then what did they bring for dessert?"

He laughed. "Homemade peach ice cream."

"Then, those pies can wait." She headed to the freezer.

~~~

It was late when Christie finally stuck the pecan pies in the pie safe, but it was okay with her. She enjoyed the quiet of the evenings. From her spot on the glider under the trees, she could see the flicker of the television set as her father
~~~

watched a classic western feature. She stood and stretched, deciding to walk down to the barn. Checking the water in the trough, the horses ambled up to her. She stroked the mare's side. "What do you say, old girl? Too many questions and not enough answers?"

The horse neighed.

"Yep, exactly what I was thinking."

That night, Christie tossed and turned, sleep evading her.

Was Hector having an affair with Kimberly? Had he called it off, and she'd gotten mad? Or was their argument about him telling Cole? Or something else entirely? It was possible that his death could be from natural causes or heatstroke. But then, why would he have driven out to their place if he felt so ill?

Another thought intruded. Kimberly cheating on Cole...where did she fit in the picture? She would have wanted to stop Hector from telling Cole about it but Hector coming to their place didn't fit.

Cole had been out on the property. He could

have picked up her phone and texted Hector to come out, then confronted Hector. But Hector hadn't been attacked, so that made little sense. Maybe he wanted to find out if Hector was having an affair with Kimberly but decided against confronting him and simply didn't show up. Yet he had been adamant that they take the money offered by the Websters for Pop's accident.

Christie laid on her back and wiggled her fingers on her hand that had fallen asleep. She sighed. The fact remained that the people who had the most to gain would be the Websters.

They had a lot to lose if Hector implicated them in the Altgelt fire. They would lose everything. People have killed for much less. But again, nothing pointed to Hector dying from anything other than natural causes—either heatstroke or—. Christie shot up in bed. The electrolyte drinks. Both Cole and Hector were drinking it and Cole had complained of a stomach-ache.

"Ugh. Stop it. You're making things up." Christie flipped her pillow to the cool side and punched it down. She turned over and faced toward the back of the sofa. She needed to sleep in a real bed. The couch had been comfortable enough for a day or two, but after that, Christie struggled to get comfortable and her back was starting to complain. She needed to talk to Pop about a different arrangement when she visited.

She thought of her father. At his age he couldn't handle this place much longer on his own. She'd noticed him having lapses with his memory and had caught him sleeping on the porch with a lit cigar close by. It was a vice he'd tried to give up for years, but he had taken it back up when her mother died. Christie always knew when Pop's stress levels increased because he caved into smoking. Thankfully, she'd noticed him going back to it less while she'd been back home. But his injury hadn't helped. He knew she disapproved so he'd often do it while she was away from home.

She struggled with the thoughts of her father's growing need for help. It may be that she would need to consider coming back home to care for her father. She would, of course. In an instant. But she couldn't live here. Christie sighed deeply and took deep breaths. Maybe tomorrow they'd get some answers.

Chapter Seven

Christie retrieved one of the pecan pies from the pie safe. The pecans glistened in their sea of syrup. She recalled how she'd found out that when the pie was first made, it had been called syrup pie. Then someone added pecans to it. She covered the pie with a beeswax wrap, and settling it into the seat, she drove over to the address in Boerne that Trish had provided her.

Hector's house was in the older section of town where many homes bore yellowed limestone along the lower portion of the outside facades. She drove down Main Street, passing many familiar establishments and some new shops that caught her eye before turning on to Hector's street. As Christie turned the corner, she spied Trish waving from her truck.

Christie pulled up at the curb behind Trish and got out. "You been waiting long?"

Trish bounced over. "Nope. Just got here, too. Need a hand?"

"No, thanks. Got it." Christie opened the back door and retrieved the pie container. They walked past a stand of crepe myrtle on their approach to the front door and rang the doorbell. The door opened, and a young woman wearing a baggie t-shirt with the Texas star emblazoned on it and cut-off denim shorts answered the door. She wore her dirty blonde hair up in a high ponytail. Christie guessed the woman to be in her early twenties.

"Hey, Trish. Come on in." The woman switched a washcloth to her other hand and opened the screen door.

"Thanks for letting us stop by, Shana May. This is my friend, Christie. She's the one I told you about who makes this to-die-for pie."

"Sounds yummy. I'm about to take a break anyway. Let's go to the kitchen." Christie and Trish followed the woman back to a small kitchen. The house wasn't much bigger than her father's place.

As Trish and Shana May conversed, Christie

asked, "Is it okay if I use the bathroom?"

"Sure. Normally, I'd say I couldn't since it's not my house, but with Hector...it's just so sad." Shana May teared up and pointed to the right. She took a deep breath before replying, "It's just past the living room."

Christie entered a hallway that was only long enough to have three doors. She peeked into the front room and saw that it was being used as an office. Papers were piled in a wire tray, and a computer's black screen revealed nothing. She'd love to look around in there but didn't want Shana May to get suspicious. She turned to the door on the other end of the hallway.

The modest bedroom at the back of the house included a queen bed and two antique nightstands. The tiny room was clean, and Christie guessed Hector had a chest of drawers in the closet. But first, the nightstands. One side of the bed was clearly his side. A Yeti cup with a Whataburger logo sat next to the bed. Another wide-mouth bottle of indeterminate color made Christie gag. She never could understand snuff. A can of the chewing tobacco sat on top of the alarm clock radio. Other than that, the top of the bedside table was clear. She drew closer to his side and eased open the top drawer, in case it made any noise. She rifled through it, but nothing seemed out of the ordinary.

Christie listened for a moment and heard the women laughing. Trish was doing her job of keeping the woman interested in the discussion. She quickly went around to the other side. Hand lotion and some other woman's things proved that a woman had slept here at some point. She couldn't go through it now though. She wished she had time to check out the closet, but time was ticking away.

She peeked around the corner of the bedroom door, then scurried into the bathroom. Once in the room, she shut the door and opened the medicine cabinet. Inside were standard items, like ibuprofen tablets, shaving cream, toothpaste, and other toiletries. It didn't look like Hector had been on any medication. Christie had seen nothing like that in the bedroom or the kitchen. Hector must not have been afflicted with any major disease or took any meds unless he kept them in the kitchen or with him. That meant that whatever had killed him had been given to him or he'd had heatstroke. But Christie knew that was a remote possibility. Hector had been driving in an air-conditioned truck. His shirt did not bear the signs of sweat under his arms or around his collar. That meant that something he ingested had caused the issue. Now if she could only figure out what that something had been.

Christie opened the door quietly, and when she heard the women still talking, she went over to the office. On the desk, a parcel map and other documents were stacked in a tray. Shana May's voice called out. "You okay in there?"

Christie jumped.

Shoot. I've got to hurry.

She snuck back into the bathroom and flushed the toilet. As she went into the kitchen, she moaned and rubbed her stomach. "Sorry. I felt like I would be sick. But nothing. Must have been something I ate."

"Oh, sorry to hear that." Shana May took a bite of the pie. "This pie is delish."

"Thanks. I like to serve with a scoop of Blue Bell homemade vanilla ice cream."

"Yum. You don't want any?"

Christie shook her head and rubbed her tummy. "Do you think Hector has any milk in the fridge? I hate to bother, but it might settle my stomach." She didn't acknowledge Trish rolling her eyes at her stunt.

Shana May hopped up. "Let me check."

Christie rushed over to the fridge. "Oh, I can do it."

Inside, she saw the expected contents of a bachelor's refrigerator—a box from a local pizza shop, bottles of Shiner Bock, and a bunch of electrolyte drinks in various colors.

Shana May joined her at the fridge. "Here. You could have one of these."

A thought popped into Christie's mind. "No! Stop. Don't touch it."

The woman turned and looked at Christie. "Um, o—kay."

"Sorry. I—" The young woman frowned and cocked her head, which instantly reminded Christie of a young friend she knew in Colorado.

"Listen, Shana May, I'm going to level with you."

Shana May plopped into the spindle back chair and stared up at Christie.

Christie closed the fridge, and not seeing but two chairs, leaned against the tiled kitchen counter. "We think Hector's death is suspicious."

"Suspicious, like, how?" Shana May folded her arms and looked back and forth between the women.

"It just seems weird, that's all," Christie said. "Hector was young, and for him to die of no apparent cause, it just seems—"

"Oh, gotcha. Yeah, that is, like, weird." Her mobile phone rang. She held up a finger. "Hello. Shana May here," she chirped. She listened. Nodded. "Um, hum. Okay." She ended the call.

"Hate to be a spoilsport, but I have to get back to work. That was Tyler Webster. They will be stopping by and wondered if I would be here."

"Okay. Well, thanks for letting us visit." Trish hugged Shana May.

Christie waved at her. "Nice meeting you."

The young woman stood on her tiptoes and hugged Christie. "Thanks for the pie. That was, like, delicious."

"You're welcome." She smiled at yet another reminder of her young friend's habit of using *like* in her sentences.

They moved out to the street. Trish spoke first. "You little snoop. What did you find?"

"Stop. I already feel horrible sneaking around like that. But if they think I or my Pop had anything to do with Hector's death, I feel like I need to get some answers."

"Okay, you're forgiven." Trish crossed her arms. "So, spill."

"Hector was definitely involved with a woman."

"Noooo," Trish whispered. "The gall of that man. A young bachelor, and he had a girlfriend!" She feigned shock and put her hand over her mouth. Then, she said, "Whatever is the world coming to?"

"Ha. Ha." Christie pursed her lips. "But it's the lotion. I think it's like what Kimberly uses. I saw some like it in her basket at the grocery store the other day. There was also a bottle of essential oil in the bathroom."

"Ah. Now we're getting somewhere. She's been trying to get me to buy that stuff forever." Trish leaned against Christie's Jeep. "But everyone uses oils nowadays. Again, not really any proof."

"Okay, I also saw a parcel map on Hector's desk. I didn't have time to look at it."

"What about drawers? Anything in the desk?"

Christie shook her head. "I didn't have time."

"Ohhhh." Trish bent over. "Not feeling so good."

"Are you okay?" Christie put an arm around her friend.

"I'm fine. I'm just putting on a show in case the neighbors are watching."

Christie looked up as a curtain in a neighbor's front window fell back in place. She gritted through her teeth. "Don't do that. You scared me to death."

"Why?" Trish rose but kept her hand on her stomach.

"I think I know how Hector was killed."

Trish bolted upright. "Killed? For real?"

"Yes. For real. Killed."

"How?"

"Antifreeze."

Trish responded with a shocked expression. "Oh. My. Gravy. You're really good. How did you figure that out?"

"The bottles of electrolyte drinks. Think about it. Hector was sick to his stomach. Then he acted drunk. I thought it might be low blood sugar or heatstroke, but that's also a sign of Ethylene Glycol poisoning."

"Huh?"

"Antifreeze."

"Whoa. Shana May had said Hector had not been feeling well the last few days. He'd started drinking more of those drinks, but it hadn't seemed to help." Trish stopped. "Poor Hector. It shouldn't have happened to him."

"We've got to go to the police and let them know. But first, one of us will have to stay here and make sure Shana May doesn't drink any of it."

"Not to worry about that. She hates that stuff. She's never understood how anyone drinks that chemical... well, I won't say what else she calls it. She's into natural things."

"Okay, well, I'm going to the sheriff with my suspicions. What do you plan on doing?"

"I'm sick, too, remember? Must be some stomach bug going around. I will go use Hector's bathroom and see what else I can find in the office."

Christie sighed. "I felt so guilty and weird going through his stuff."

Trish laughed. "You forget, I'm the mom of a teenage boy. I go through stuff all the time."

"Isn't that an invasion of privacy?"

"Yes. But I'd rather invade his privacy than to find out he's involved in drugs or something else. If you were a mom, you'd understand."

Was that an underhanded dig? No, I'm just

on edge.

"I guess. Well, I better get going." Christie slid into her car and turned the AC up to high. She waved and pulled away from the curb as Trish walked back up to the house. As she drove around the corner, a white pickup headed toward her.

Shoot. Must be Tyler Webster.

But as the truck pulled up alongside her, she saw that it was Cole. He slowed down his truck and waved at her to lower her window.

"Christie."

"Cole."

"What are you doing in this part of town?"

"Well, it's not really any of your business, but I was visiting a friend."

"Christie, what's with you?"

"What do you mean?"

"You act like I've offended you, and I don't know how. I thought, after all these years, we could be friends again." He gripped his steering wheel.

Christie took a deep breath and let it out.

"Sorry. I've just been on edge with my father's injury, then Hector dying on our property—"

"No apology necessary. How's your Pop doing?"

"Cantankerous as ever." Christie grinned.

Cole retorted, "He's always been nice to me. Listen, I really want to talk to you about the Webster proposal. I know your dad said no, but I'd at least like to give you the full story."

"Oh, so that's what you mean about being friends? You want to try to cozy up to me to get to my Pop."

"No. I never said—"

"I have to get going." She raised her window.

What was she thinking? Cole was only being friendly so he could work his old charms on her. And she'd almost fallen for it.

~~~

After talking with the sheriff's deputy about her suspicions, she left dejected after he told her they couldn't pursue her theory simply on a
~~~

"hunch." Even when she'd informed him of a similar instance where someone had given an elderly relative antifreeze in their drink, the deputy had insinuated that Christie knew an awful lot about how it could kill. She left more frustrated than ever. At least he said he would talk to the medical examiner. It was out of her hands.

Her phone chirped.

"Pop?" Is everything okay?" She heard Mutt and Jeffrey barking.

"Yep. Them dumb dogs don't bark at anything else. But see a squirrel, and you'd a thought the squirrel was trying to burglarize the place. When are you coming to take me over to see Curtis?"

"I'm on my way now."

"All right."

The line went dead.

Once she arrived home, Pop agreed to letting her take the other pecan pie over to Curtis if she'd bake him another one. They needed to retrieve more hay for the mare and the foal, and Curtis still had some in a covered lean-to.

As they drove, Pop spoke, "Oh, I found your

phone."

"You did? Where?"

"It was on the ground outside. It must have fallen out there by the tree. I walked by it and saw it."

"That's weird. Why wouldn't we have seen it earlier? And how could it have been missed?"

Christie slammed on the brakes causing Pop to grab for the dashboard.

"What the—"

"Pop! You didn't pick it up with your hands?"

"Well, of course I did. Whatcha expect me to pick it up with? My toes?"

Christie slammed her hand against the steering wheel. Whoever had used her phone to text Hector had surely wiped the phone of prints, and now the only prints that would be on the phone would be Pop's. That wouldn't look good.

"Pop. I think that Hector was killed. Whoever texted him used my phone. They're trying to make it look like I—or even you—had something to do with it. So at some point that same person brought the phone back to the property."

"Well if that don't beat all. Someone better not be messing with my girl. No siree."

Chapter Eight

They drove over to the Altgelt ranch in silence. As they made their way up the dirt road, Christie spied a Mercedes parked out in front. Two men looked up as the truck headed toward them. Christie maneuvered the truck up to the corral next to the charred remains of the barn.

"Daggum shame. That's what that is. Curtis loved that barn." Pop shook his head.

Christie got out of the truck and opened the passenger side door for her father. He cradled his hurt arm as he exited the vehicle.

One of the men picked up a map like the one she'd seen at Hector's.

Pop stretched. "What are you boys doing out here?"

"I don't see how that's any of your business, old man." The taller of the two men stepped forward.

Pop sighed deeply. He moved closer to the taller man. "This is Curtis's place. So, I'll ask you again. Does Curtis know you're out here?"

Christie stood by, her stomach in a knot. Surely, these men weren't going to pick a fight with her father.

"We have as much right to be here as you do." The man with the map rolled it up. "Plus, once he's gone, this will be our place."

"You know, I hate people who don't respect their elders." With surprising speed for his age, Pop reached over, grabbed the map out of the man's hand, threw it down, and ground it into the dirt with the heel of his boot.

"Old man, I'm going—" The man in the blue shirt took a step toward Pop.

Christie stepped forward. "If I were you, I would rethink what you're planning."

"Or what?" He sneered. "Who's going to stop me? You? That pitiful old man with his arm in a sling?"

"Don't say I didn't warn you." Christie replied.

A high-pitch scream sounded as the man dropped to his knees.

Pop had hold of the man's hand, and every time he tried to get up from his knees, Pop pressed again.

"Stop! Stop it!" The man took a swing, only hitting air.

"Now, see here. First, you don't respect your elders. Then, no one, and I mean no one, talks to my Christie like that."

"You're insane." He tried to take a swing again but cried out in pain as Pop added more pressure to the man's hand.

"Sonny, you need to behave. I won't put up with those kinds of people who need to be scraped off the bottom of my shoe." He moved, and the man crawled after him, his once crisply starched, gray slacks now covered in dirt.

The other man took a step forward. Pop squeezed the man's hand again.

"Stay there, Erik!" The man gestured with his free hand.

Pop moved them around until the man faced

Christie. "You say you're sorry now, son."

"Sorry."

Pop squeezed. "That don't sound sincere, like."

"I'm sorry."

He looked up at Pop, who waited.

The man spoke to Christie, "I apologize for my words, ma'am."

"Better." He stood there for a minute. "Now, if I let you loose, are you going to be a good boy?"

"Yes."

Erik took another step. "Nick said he was sorry. Now let him up."

"Don't let this arm fool ya, now, son."

"Erik, move away."

A truck drove up. Curtis got out, and a smile played on his lips.

"What's going on here?"

"Ahh nothing. We came over to get that hay, and Christie brought you one of her famous pecan pies."

"Let's go inside, and I'll put on the pot."

The man on the ground pointed at Pop. "Are

you going to make him stop?"

"Oh, no. Nick, it seems like you must have done something to make R.C. almost mad."

"Almost mad?"

He laughed. "Yep. You don't want to see R.C. actually mad."

Pop looked down at the man. "Son, you going to behave now?"

"I already said I...yes, sir."

Pop let go of Nick's hand.

Erik helped Nick up, then said, "Can you teach me how to do that?"

"Sure," responded Pop. "Give me your hand."

"Um, no thanks." He backed away. "Nick, let's get out of here."

Nick rubbed his hand as he climbed into the passenger side of the car. Erik gunned the Mercedes, and in a last act of defiance, he spun out on the gravel before he headed back down the road.

Inside, Curtis put on the coffee, and the trio gathered around the scarred oak table in the dining room. When they each had a cup of coffee and pie in front of them, Curtis spoke. "I loved their mother. God rest her soul. I took them boys in like they were my own. Then, they moved off and went to live with their father. Now, they're like buzzards flying over me, looking for my dead body."

So, that's why the pair looked familiar. Though, when she had known them, they had both been short and plump. Christie knew better than to interrupt, but she wondered why Curtis didn't just cut them out of his will.

As if he'd read her mind, Curtis continued. "I told their mother I'd always treat them like they were my own. I made her a promise."

"Yes, but that was when they were kids." Christie took a sip of the strong, bitter coffee.

"True, enough. But I need to stand by my word."

"What would Marilyn have wanted?"

"I know she'd have been unhappy about how them boys turned out." He shook his head.

Pop interrupted Curtis. "Christie has some news."

She swallowed a sip of the hot brew. "I do?"

"The fence?"

"Oh, yeah. When Trish and I were out riding on our property, we noticed that the fence had been cut between our properties and the main wood post pulled up."

"Where is this?"

"The old animal track on the back forty."

"Interesting."

"Why?"

"Tyler Webster's been coming around, asking about the property. I've told him over and over, I'm not ready to sell. Then, he contacted the boys. Not sure how he did that. After that, I've been noticing strange things happening around here."

Christie set her cup down on the table, "Like what?"

"Stuff in the shed that's always on the right side was down on the left side. I'd go back later, and the items were back in the right place. Then, I found my remote in the fridge." He sighed. "It sucks getting older and losing your mind. But now, I wonder."

Christie was familiar with patients who suffered from dementia or Alzheimer's. She'd cared for many of them in their last days. "Have you seen a doctor lately?"

The men laughed. "For what? Getting old?" Pop asked.

"Pop, it's good to get a diagnosis if there's an issue."

"No issue. If I leave something in the wrong place, then I just have to find it."

"Have you been experiencing this, too?" she asked Pop.

He patted her hand. "Don't worry, darling. It's all just part and parcel of getting older...except..."

"Except what?"

"I could have sworn I put that—"

Christie's new phone rang. "Excuse me." She went into the other room. It was Trish.

"Hey. What's up?" Christie put the phone on speaker.

"Christie. It's all gone."

"What do you mean?"

"Shana May called me and let me know that Emma and Kimberly came in and went through the place like a tornado. It's all gone. Everything."

"What?"

"Yep. Turns out Hector was renting the place from the Websters, and they wanted it cleaned out so they could have it ready to rent for the first of the month. They took most of the stuff to the thrift store and boxed up his stuff."

"But what about his family?"

"His parents live in Mexico. They're trying to reach them now."

"Wait. What about the electrolyte drinks?"

"They threw them all away."

Christie moaned. "I guess that's it, then. We tried."

"I've got worse news."

"Worse than that?" Christie tucked her hair behind her ear.

"Yeppers. Remember Mike's friend, the cop? Turns out, the cause of Hector's death has been ruled inconclusive."

"If they would just test his blood chemical—"

"Not sure what they did. Plus, he's going to be cremated. So, that looks like the end of that."

"Oh, geez. I don't want this hanging over our heads forever. Plus, Hector deserves justice."

"Christie, I really think you should let this go."

"We've got to get those bottles. When's trash day?"

"Day after tomorrow. Why?"

"You up for stealing some trash?"

Trish laughed. "Are you turning into a criminal?"

"Listen, I'm not at home but I'll call you later."

Chapter Nine

"Don't you think they moved awfully fast? I mean, Hector just died." Christie plopped down on the sofa back at the house. "It makes me wonder if Emma or Tyler aren't involved in Hector's death."

"I don't know. Hearts of gold, those two have."

Christie snorted into the phone. "Tell me what you really think."

Trish continued, "In simple terms, if it isn't making them money, they don't care. It's close to the end of the month, so I'm sure they want the house ready for renting on the first of next month, is my guess."

Christie thought for a moment. "Let's think about this. Didn't Marie say it was rumored that Hector was having an affair with a married woman?"

"Yeah." She heard Trish whisper to someone,

"Not that one. The one in the fridge."

"Do you need to get off the phone?"

"No. My bad. I hate when people do that. Ya know? Two conversations at once. But I've got Jess on dinner tonight."

"Good for you, having him cook."

"He loves it. Plus, it won't be long before he's out on his own. It's a basic skill all kiddos should learn."

"You're a great mom, Trish."

"Ahhh, that's so sweet, Christie." Pans clanging interrupted her. "Hold on. I'm going in the other room so I can put you on speaker while I fold some laundry."

Christie waited as she heard Trish move through the house, then say, "Guess what? It's now the talk of the town that Kimberly's been having an affair with Hector."

"Do you remember the old telephone game?"

"You mean, one person tells something to start, and at the end, it's completely different? Yeah, sort of. I think we played that in, like, third grade."

"Ugh. You're making me feel old now." Christie switched the phone to her other ear. "What if...just conjecture here...but what if someone heard from someone else that Hector was having an affair? They probably wouldn't spill names because they wouldn't want the rumors getting back to them. But what if they 'hinted' that it was a petite blonde?"

"Whoa." She heard Trish plop down onto her bed. "That makes so much sense. We only found a woman's things at Hector's. The Websters came and got everything out of that house like it was on fire. Let's think about this."

"I thought that was what we were doing."

"Ha, ha. Okay, so maybe Hector was having an affair with Emma, not Kimberly. Tyler finds out and puts antifreeze in his electrolyte drink. Then, he lures Hector out to y'all's place because there's no phone service in that area. Done. Revenge."

"Okay. Good thoughts. But how did Tyler get my phone? And, why would he try to implicate me in Hector's crime? He doesn't even know me."

"Hmmmm." Trish squealed. "I am so good. I got it. He changes his mind, but it's too late. He confides in Emma and says they have to get the drink away from Hector. Emma, who's been caught out, knows which side of her bed—I mean, bread, is buttered. Tyler owns the company. She'd lose everything. So she tries to get the drinks out of Hector's truck. He sees her, and they have that knock-down, drag-out at the café. It could have been her and not Kimberly he had been speaking to right before Hector left."

Christie interjected. "Interesting. But what you're implying is that she went along with covering up an attempted murder. Plus, remember at this point, nothing had happened. Hector hadn't drunk any of the drink. Or at least that we know of. Well, maybe he had, but it only made him ill. Remember how he'd not been feeling well. Plus, I hate to say it, but what about Cole?"

"Cole? What's he got to do with this!" Trish's voice jumped with emotion.

"What if he wanted Hector out of the way so he could get the commission on our place? Or for that matter, the Altgelt place."

"No way. Not Cole. But if Kimberly had been having an affair—"

Christie responded, "I think we're just going in circles. Nothing makes sense."

"On another note, heard you met Curtis's stepsons."

"How—"

"Small town. They were at Mary's Taco's in one of the little rooms, but Marie said she heard them talking. Seems they're not too happy with your Pop."

"They're a piece of work, for sure. I wouldn't put it past them to have burned down the barn to get Curtis to move. They had a map like the one in Hector's office. I wish I could have gotten a better look before Cole, or whoever, came and got it."

"Well..." Trish sighed.

"Spill it."

"Maybe someone just borrowed it and a few other things from Hector's desk."

"You stole the map?"

"I borrowed it, thank you very much. Plus,

they've got to have copies."

Christie moaned. "Ugh, I can't believe—"

"Hey, do you want to see it or not? I am trying to help you and Pop out, ya know?"

"I know. I appreciate it. But I also don't want my friend ending up in jail for theft."

"Least of my worries. Anyway, borrowed."

"Okay. Borrowed. But how do you plan to give it back?" Christie grabbed a piece of paper and started a to-do list.

"Yeah, them cleaning out the place put a bit of a kink in my plans."

Christie laughed. "Ya think?"

"I'll figure it out. I always do."

"Okay, so back to our theory. Tyler either decides to warn Hector off or kill him. But how did he get my phone to text Hector?" Christie jotted down a reminder.

"We don't know if he did. So, what we need to figure out is when the phone disappeared. Think back. When was the last time you saw your phone?"

Christie thought about it. "Um, I had it at

Pop's. The last time I remember seeing it was after I had finished a call with a mechanic about bringing my Jeep in for some work next week or so. Dad was getting in his truck. I dropped my phone in the console and went over and told him I'd see him later. Then, I forgot it when we were inside eating lunch."

"Did you lock your car that day?"

"I never lock it. It's an old car. I have nothing in it anyone would want." Christie added 'tires' to her list.

"Except your phone."

"Yeah, there's that. But you saw it. It wasn't even a smart phone. It was an old flip style phone—basically calls and texts only. I used my work phone for almost everything, and I left it there when I came out here."

Trish answered her, "Okay, you left your car unlocked and you've been in all kinds of parking lots, where anyone in the entire Kendall county area could have taken it."

Christie moaned. "True. Bummer. I guess anyone—Hector, Kimberly, anyone really—could have taken it. Then, when the truck hit Pop, I totally forgot about it until later."

"So, that means, once Emma or Tyler heard about the accident, they could have come out to your place after Jess returned your car. They could have taken it to look at and forgot to put it back. It would be easy to go there while you all are at the doctor's. They may have wanted to see if you'd contacted a lawyer."

"A lawyer? My Pop was injured. I couldn't have cared less about money."

"But you forget. Their hearts are made of gold. Oh, geez, smoke alarm. Gotta run!"

Christie set down her new smartphone she'd bought when her old phone got lost.

I can't believe I spent that much money on a stupid phone.

Her mind wandered. If Hector had planned to leave the company, maybe Emma was afraid he would tell Tyler about their affair. She couldn't have that. While Tyler could have found out and gone after Hector, it didn't add up. Unfortunately, it didn't put Cole free and clear, either. They were just assuming the affair was with Kimberly and not with Emma.

A knock on the front door startled Christie. She'd been deep in thought and hadn't even heard the truck approaching. Where were Mutt and Jeffrey when she needed them? She wondered if she could pretend she wasn't home.

"I know you're in there, Christie!" Kimberly shouted as the knocking intensified. "Please open the door. I need to speak to you."

Christie opened the door and stepped outside.

Kimberly wore cut-off jeans, a halter top with a ripped t-shirt on top that said 'Diva-Queen,' and flip flops with rhinestones. Her newly highlighted blonde hair was piled on top of her head in a messy bun. Her makeup looked fresh.

"I'm sorry I look like such a mess."

Again with the fishing for compliments. Now that she thought about it, Kimberly had been like that her entire life. What did Cole see in her? Well, duh, she was cute and hot at the same time, something Christie knew she would never, ever be.

"Can we sit?" Kimberly smiled, showing her expensive, straight pearly whites.

Christie motioned to a rocker and took the farthest chair. Where *were* Mutt and Jeffrey? It wasn't like them to not jump at the chance for pets or treats. "What can I help you with, Kimberly?"

Kimberly remained standing after looking at the old, worn rocker. She pushed a lock of hair from her forehead. "Listen, I came over to apologize." She smiled.

"Continue." Christie sat back in the chair and tried not to be distracted but kept scanning the property for the two dogs.

Kimberly huffed. "Don't you think you owe me an apology, too? After all, I wouldn't have reacted the way I did if you—"

"Wait a cotton-picking minute." Christie bristled. "Basically, you're not apologizing for your atrocious behavior, then?"

"I said I was sorry I got mad after you—"

"No, that's a 'but' apology. It's not *if* I wouldn't have done something to cause your reaction. That's not a real apology. That's a deflection back onto me."

Kimberly bristled and took a step back. "Well, I'm sorry that you seem to have a problem with saying you're sorry."

"I don't have a problem with it. I'm not sorry. Therefore, no apology."

"Well, I never."

"I bet that's true. Or not. Depending on what we're talking about."

Kimberly harrumphed, "You've changed, Christie. You used to be so nice in high school."

"I guess you could say that. I grew up. I look at things as an adult now."

Kimberly crossed her arms. "I can't help you if—"

"What gives you the impression that I need help?" She turned from Kimberly and yelled out, "Mutt! Jeffrey! Here boys!"

Kimberly hissed, "Just stay away from Cole."

That blindsided Christie, and she turned back to Kimberly. "I beg your pardon?"

"You heard me." She thrust her chin out.

"High school crushes are over, and he's mine now."

"Wow. Just...wow." Christie crossed her arms over her chest and shook her head, a laugh escaping her lips. "I'm not going after Cole, so you can rest your airless brain. I think this conversation is over." She stood and towered over Kimberly, who took a step back.

Kimberly smiled up at Christie. "Okay. Well, I hope we can be friends during the time you're here."

What a nutty woman. An idea came to Christie.

Christie turned on the 'I'm dealing with horrible people' charm she'd often used while working with hospice patients or their family members. She sat down and started her act. "I'm sorry. I'm just dealing with Pop's accident and Hector's death on our property. It's a lot, ya know?"

After wiping off the other rocker seat, Kimberly sat. "Ahh, come here." She reached over and hugged Christie, who stuck out her tongue behind the woman's back. Drama class had come in handy.

"I knew, deep down, you wanted to say sorry and make up."

A moment from eighth grade flashed through Christie's mind. Kimberly had a cat who loved Christie but stayed away from Kimberly most of the time. It had irritated Kimberly that the cat had liked Christie more than her. One weekend, Kimberly invited Trish and Christie and a couple of other classmates to her house for a sleepover. When Kimberly tried to pull the cat away from Christie, the cat had scratched Kimberly's hand. At the time she'd blamed Christie and said she thought she should apologize for the cat scratching her. A few days later at school, Kimberly told the girls about how her poor Fife had died and gone to heaven. She had lapped up the attention, and to Christie's knowledge, she never had a cat again.

Attention. That was it. Kimberly craved it. Had to have it. Christie knew she had to use that to find out what she needed.

As they pulled away from their embrace,

Christie feigned wiping tears from her eyes, and Kimberly patted her hand. "Ahh, honey. No need to cry. We can still be friends."

This woman was truly something. Vanity poured from her veins. Christie leaned back and thought of her next question. "Hey, Kimberly, are you good friends with Emma Webster?"

"Oh, yes. We're like this." She crossed her fingers. "We often go out to eat with Emma and Tyler over at Perry's. Their food is delicious. Why?"

Appeal to the vanity.

"Sounds like y'all are the power couples around these parts."

Kimberly beamed. "After Daddy died and left me the ranch, it helped me to do some investing on my own. I helped Tyler get started, and he agreed to bring Cole on. I've financed quite a few of the Websters projects."

"So, you're friends with Tyler?"

Kimberly shifted in her seat and licked her lips. "Mainly Emma. She and I go way back. From college days."

Christie's mind whirled. If Kimberly and

Emma were close—and who knew exactly how close—she could have easily known if they were having an affair. But were they true friends? In the Websters quest for building up their property holdings, did Kimberly feel threatened by Emma and Hector's relationship? Plus, with Hector out of the way, Cole would take his place and get a huge commission on the sales.

"Hey, Christie, how about we go horseback riding this week?"

That was the last thing she wanted to do, but she consented. Kimberly hugged her again before flouncing off toward her truck. "I'm glad we got everything straightened out, " she called out then air-kissed her hand and blew it toward Christie.

Christie returned the gesture with a wave and smile. She hated the idea of spending more time with Kimberly, but she had to get to the bottom of this. Right now, it looked like she had four clear suspects—Tyler, Emma, Cole, and Kimberly. Each had a strong motive. Emma could have a lot more to lose if she had been having an affair with Hector and was discovered. It was terrible what greed could do to a person. Yet jealousy could have caused Tyler or Cole to want revenge. Emma and Kimberly were friends but had one been envious of the other's relationship with Hector? One of them was a cold and calculating murderer, but which one?

So much to think about but for now, she needed to find Mutt and Jeffrey.

Chapter Ten

Christie walked out to the stables to see if her father was there and the dogs had tagged along with him. But no signs of either. She looked out toward a large oak tree back behind the tool shed. It was set up with a wooden table and chairs, and she smiled as she remembered playing with other children, while the parents played dominos. Those were certainly simpler times. But her father wasn't there, either. Nor were the dogs.

Now worried, Christie hurried back to the house. Had her father taken ill? She burst through the back door, the screen door slamming behind her. She looked in his bedroom, then the bathroom. Then, she saw the other room with the door ajar. Her father sat in a chair; his head cradled in his left hand. It was at that moment Christie saw how frail her father had become.

She knocked softly on the door and entered.

Kneeling in front of him, she spoke soothingly. "Pop, are you okay?"

He wiped his face to show that it wasn't tears that streaked his cheeks. He raked his hand across his grizzly beard, making a sound like sandpaper.

She gingerly grasped the hand in the sling as he smiled down at her. "Baby girl, I think it's 'bout time we got rid of some of mom's stuff. But I just can't throw it away." He shook his head. "I can't."

"Of course not, Pop. I know that the Pass It On thrift store would be happy to receive some of this stuff. I think they help kids get scholarships."

"You think they would?" He looked into her eyes to judge the sincerity.

"Yes." She smiled. "I know they would." She stood up and stretched. "I can help you with it, if you'd like."

"That'd be great." He sighed. "I'm worthless with this gimp arm."

"No you're not. Just think about how you showed Curtis's boy."

"Not one of Curtis's boys. Never will be. Glad when they left to go live with their Pa."

"On another subject, I can't find Mutt and Jeffrey. I've looked out at the stables, under the oak, by the vehicles."

"Hmm, did ya call'em?"

"I was surprised they didn't come running when Kimberly came over, or you, for that matter."

He shook his head and stood. "I couldn't handle that woman today. I knew I was gonna say something that would've made your poor Ma ashamed of me, so I just came in here." He walked through the kitchen, opened the back door, and whistled. No dogs.

"Nope. "He strode to the front and whistled again. The boys didn't come running. "Something ain't right."

"Where do you think they could have gone, Pop?"

"I reckon they been out further on the property. But they normally come a-running when I whistle. We need to go check on them." He headed for his truck. "We'll take the back track that runs through the meadow."

Christie helped Pop settle and went over and climbed up into the cab. She started the truck, and they headed out past the stables. Heat from the sun beat down on them, but they kept the windows down as she called to the dogs along the way. Every once in a while, Pop would whistle, but no happy dogs came running.

"While we're out here, we should stop by the broken fence area. I can show you what I was talking about."

"Good idea." He adjusted his old felt hat lower on his head.

They'd reached the field, when Christie heard a sound. Barking. She slammed on the brakes and turned off the vehicle. It was the boys. She slid down out of the cab and went around to open her dad's side. He whistled, but the barking only intensified.

"We got to hurry. They're trying to get us to come." He moved quickly toward the yapping.

As Christie and Pop made their way along the overgrown dirt track, Mutt came bounding up to meet them. He licked their hands and danced around excitedly. But no Jeffrey.

"I hope he hasn't got bitten by a rattler," Pop said.

"Eek. I hope not, too." Christie, who had come out in her flip flops, surveyed the ground in front of her as she walked.

"What the…" Pop upped his pace.

Christie saw Jeffrey. The chocolate lab lay next to what looked to be a pile of clothes. She quickly realized it was a person and broke into a jog. It was Curtis.

The man was unconscious but alive. She looked down at his feet. One was at an awkward angle. "Pop, it looks like he's broken his ankle. Is there any signal out here?"

Curtis moaned. Christie reached down and felt his wrist. His skin felt cold and clammy. "Pop, do you have any water in the truck?"

"I do, but it's warm."

"That's okay. Can you get it for me?"

While Pop went to gather the water, Christie assessed Curtis. His pulse was weak but steady. "Curtis, can you hear me?"

He moaned.

"It's okay. We're going to get you help." She took the water Pop handed her, poured some on a clean handkerchief of her father's, and used it to wipe his face and hairline where blood had collected. He must have hit his head when he stumbled into that hole; possibly a fox or rabbit den. Hopefully, he didn't have a concussion too, but he had a nasty gash on his forehead and a big knot on his head.

"Pop, can you pull the blanket out from behind the cab? I'm going to put him in the back of the truck. You'll need to drive."

"Shouldn't we get help?"

"Yes. But by the time we get back to the house and call someone, we've wasted precious minutes. He's already in a state of shock. We need to get him help quickly."

She spoke softly to the man. "Curtis, I'm going to pick you up, and we're going to put you in the truck. I'll try to be as gentle as I can. Are you able to squeeze my hand?"

He answered with a weak squeeze.

"That's good. Now if you feel pain, you squeeze my hand or arm, okay?"

She laid out the blanket in the bed of the truck. "Okay, Pop. Go ahead and get in the truck and back it over until I stop you. Then, I'll get him in the back."

"You ain't gonna be able to lift him up in that bed."

Christie smiled. "Pop, I've helped people who weigh more than two hundred pounds during my career. Taking a one-hundred-fifty-pound, soaking wet, old man less than a yard won't be an issue."

Pop got in the truck and backed it into the grass until Christie held up her hand.

"Now this is the hard part, Curtis. You ready?" She'd torn up part of her tee-shirt and made sure his leg was secure. Gingerly, she moved him until she was able to get his arm around her back and hers around his waist. "On three. One, two…" She hoisted him up in one quick motion. Christie grunted as she moved him toward the truck. Carefully, she laid him on the blanket and climbed in with him. Jeffrey hopped into the bed with her and licked her face.

She hugged the chocolate lab's neck. "Yes, good boy." She rubbed his head, his tongue lolling. Mutt barked and jumped up into the bed with them. "You, too."

She hit the side of the truck and Pop eased the truck forward and back onto the main track.

As Christie held the man's hand, she looked back at the scene. Yes, it could have been a hole she hadn't seen the other day, but she would have definitely seen that pile of rocks as big as a cairn. Maybe Curtis was coming out to fix the fence. But she hadn't seen tools or his truck. He could have brought the rocks out earlier, but they were in a weird place. And an awfully convenient one if someone tripped and fell. In fact, the large pile of rocks could have made a very convenient way to harm or even, murder someone and make it look like an accident. If she hadn't have seen that there were no rocks there before, and Curtis had died, no one would be the wiser.

It turned out Curtis had a concussion and surgery would be needed to stabilize his ankle. He would be in the hospital for a while. He had also been severely dehydrated, and the doctor took Christie aside and told her that they had saved his life. After they saw Curtis in the hospital, they drove back home where a Webster truck idled in front of the house.

"Ugh. This people keep showing up like the plague." Christie moaned, but as they pulled closer, a man got out of his truck.

Cole waited while Christie pulled their vehicle under the shade of the oaks and turned off the ignition. She didn't know if she had the mental or emotional capacity to deal with Cole or anything to do with the Websters right now, but she steadied herself and stepped from the truck. After helping her father out, the old man walked over and shook Cole's hand.

"How you are doing, son?"

"Doing well, sir. Sorry to hear about Curtis."

Pop nodded his head and patted Cole on the shoulder. "I'm gonna go on inside. Christie will help you."

He shuffled up the steps and into the house. Christie and Cole watched him until the door shut behind him.

"How's your dad doing?" Cole asked.

"Let's see." She ticked off with her fingers. "One, you all keep trying to get him to sell the land we've had in our family for generations. Two, he was hurt badly— almost killed—again by one of you. Three, one of your people died on our property, and they've as much as accused us as being involved somehow. And finally, his friend almost died this morning and may have if we hadn't found him."

Cole held his hands up. "Whoa. I have nothing to do with any of those things."

"Yes, but I bet you're here on behalf of the Websters again."

"Okay. I get that you're upset. I would be, too, in your shoes. But don't shoot the messenger." He stuck one thumb in his jeans. "But I'm not here for that. I wanted to speak with you."

"I've got to go check on the mare and her foal.

If you want, you can walk with me."

He nodded.

They walked in silence until they came to the stables. Christie topped off the water tank, and they watched as the foal emulated the mare by trotting around the corral.

"Christie"

"Cole."

They broke out in unison.

"You go first." He motioned.

Christie leaned back, her hands on the fence post. "You came here, so what do you want to talk to me about?"

"I wanted to apologize for how I behaved the other day. I was out of line. When I heard the news about Hector, it really upset me, and you were the first person I saw. That's not an excuse. I just goofed."

"Okay. Apology accepted."

Certainly, better than Kimberly's fake attempt.

She started walking toward the creek and the shade of the Cyprus trees. Once they were in the shade, she turned to Cole. "Are you involved with trying to get Curtis's place?"

"I work for the Websters, so in that case, then, yeah."

"Let me see your hands." Christie gestured.

Cole held out his hands. The simple gold band on his left hand stood out. "What?"

"I just wanted to see how dirty they are."

"Oh, funny. Ha. Ha." He stuffed his hands into his pockets. "Look, people may not like developers and real estate people, but they don't complain when they're visiting their new favorite restaurant, shopping at a trendy store, or enjoying the view from their new patio."

Christie huffed. "I understand that. But how about focusing on in-fill. Quit trying to buy up unspoiled land from people who don't want to sell."

"Can we change the subject?"

"Okay. What do you want to talk about?"

He kicked a clod of dirt with his cowboy boot. "I'm really thinking about Hector's death. Something seems off."

She faced him. "In what way?"

"Hector was closing in on a pretty big deal. He told me it would allow him to start his own company. Now they won't have to pay him the commission." He bent down and picked up some rocks.

"But what about his estate? He has to have family somewhere."

Cole tossed a rock into the creek. It sunk and ripples shown on the surface of the water. "I'm sure. But it's not like they're going to spend time, effort, or—"

"Money," Christie finished his sentence.

"Yes, money on finding them." He picked up another rock.

Christie crossed her arms. "So, they'll keep it until someone comes looking for it."

"Which, they never will." He skipped a rock across the surface of the water.

Christie made a face. "And yet, you work for these people, who pretty much took everything and gave it away before he was even cold in the ground."

"It's a long story."

"I'll bet."

He shifted and looked at her. "You never told me what you wanted to say."

Christie turned toward the creek and watched as the water gurgled over tree roots and rocks. "I just wanted to let you know that, even though I held a grudge for a long time, I'm over that now. I hope we can be on better terms from this moment on." She faced him. "Friends again."

His brow tightened, and he frowned. "If anyone should hold a grudge from back then, it should be me."

"Whatever for?"

"You never showing up!"

"What do you mean? I'm the one who waited for you!"

Kimberly.

For all these years, she'd thought Cole had rejected her, and he thought she'd rejected him.

"Oh, geez. She played us like a violin." Christie walked over and sat on a large trunk.

Cole followed.

He reached over and took Christie's hand. "I

never would have hurt you. You should know that."

She pulled her hand away as a noise caught her attention. "Did you hear that?"

"No. I didn't hear anything. Christie, I'm sorry. If I would have known—"

"But you still ended up marrying her. Why, Cole? What do...*did*...you see in her?"

"It's complicated. When I thought you'd dumped me, Kimberly came in and worked her charm on me. By the time I realized what kind of manipulator she was, she already had her hooks in me. You know that snake in Jungle Book with the mesmerizing eyes?" He rolled his eyes and made a goofy face, causing Christie to break out in laughter.

"You're such a goof," she chuckled. "Continue."

"It wasn't too long after that, she announced our engagement. I hadn't even asked her, but I just got swept up in it. Her daddy was going to help pay for my schooling and help me get started in my business. My parents were over the moon with Kimberly. She could do no wrong in their eyes. So we got married. Everything was fine for a while, but I wasn't making good money, and she was always going to her dad for more money. More wants, more pressure to do more, be more. She's all about how things look to the outside world." He stopped for a moment. "I take that back. How *she* looks to the outside world."

"Cole, why are you telling me this? She's your wife, and I have to say, you're not speaking very highly of her."

He took his cap off and put it on his knee. "You're right. I shouldn't. But I need to talk to someone. For so many years, you were that someone. You never judged me. Just listened. Our friendship was...*is*...something I treasure." He brushed his eyebrows with his fingers and placed his cap back on his head. "Truth is, I would leave now if I could. I know if I even think about it, bad things happen."

"What do you mean?"

"Not long after we were married, I said I'd had enough, I was leaving. But she found out she was pregnant with twins. I said I'd work on our marriage and we went to counseling in San Antonio, where no one would know us. During that time, she made out as this totally different person. She manipulated the counselor like she'd done with me. Waste of time. Then, she went to her daddy and asked him to foot the bill for a house she wanted built. He'd finally had enough. He put his foot down." Cole stroked the stubble on his chin. "You know that old saying, 'hell hath no fury?' That's Kimberly when she doesn't get what she wants."

"So, she had to accept she wasn't going to get the house of her dreams?"

He launched back and roared with laughter. "You don't know her. What Kimberly wants; Kimberly gets. It was winter, and everyone got sick, but her dad got really sick. Ended up in the hospital. A few days after they released him, he died."

Chapter Eleven

Christie slapped a mosquito. "Oh, that's terrible. What was the cause of death?"

"Complications from flu." He stretched out his legs and crossed his ankles.

"Sad. How old was he?"

"Fifty-one, two. Somewhere in there."

"Was his wife with him when he died?"

"No. His wife died years earlier in a car accident. He never remarried. But Kimberly was with him in those last days, caring for him."

Christie was silent. So, Kimberly had been with him when he died, and she ended up as the sole beneficiary. She finally spoke, "I gather she got her house."

"Oh, yeah. Now that the girls are grown, we live in a five-thousand square foot house. We sleep in separate bedrooms and live our lives apart. As long as we keep up appearances to the outside world, she doesn't care."

Which makes an affair with Hector all the more likely.

"I'm sorry, Cole. I know it can be tough. I think divorce must be horrible to go through, but why didn't you leave when the girls were a bit older?"

"I tried. Trust me. But then, they became sick. Doctor visits all the time. Tests. Trying to figure out what was wrong with them. It drained me from focusing on anything but them. For Kimberly, it energized her. She received tons of sympathy, and she ate it up."

Christie repositioned herself and leaned back on the tree trunk. "You don't think she had...never mind."

"What?" He motioned for her to continue. "What were you going to say? That she played a part in their illnesses?"

"I'm just wondering if maybe she had Munchausen By Proxy. Because you said caring for the girls energized her, and the doctors couldn't figure out what was wrong, but she got lots of sympathy from other mothers, and thus, attention she craved."

"I've often wondered about it. Especially since—"

"Since what?"

"They left home. There's this exclusive boarding school in Colorado with a great equestrian program, so we sent them up there for their education. As soon as they arrived, no more problems and they thrived."

"So, they're at the school now?"

"No. That was years ago. They both live elsewhere. We rarely see them now. They're always too busy to come home for holidays and visits."

Or maybe they knew how toxic their mother was. Christie's heart ached for Cole. He'd been through so much.

He stood up. "I probably shouldn't have shared all this. I'm just at my wit's end." He grabbed her hand and pulled her up to a standing position. They locked eyes. He leaned in toward her.

"What are you doing? You're married." Christie sprang back.

"I'm sorry." Cole dropped her hand. "I thought—"

"You thought wrong. I don't know what signal you thought you were getting, but I don't kiss married men."

"I *said* I was sorry." He huffed.

She strode back toward the stables. He caught up with her. "I mean it, Christie. I don't know what I was thinking."

"Seems like you weren't thinking. First, you tell me a sob story about your life, how horrible Kimberly is, then you have the audacity to make a pass at me?" She kept walking.

He caught her arm. "Christie—"

"Remove your hand." He dropped it.

As they reached the house, she turned to him. "I think we should only see each other in a professional capacity from now on. Please call before coming out here."

"Fine."

"Fine." She crossed her arms and stood next

to the porch as he clamored into his truck and roared off down the road.

What a fool, Christie.

All the time she felt sorry for him, he was trying to put blame on Kimberly and to cause Christie to question her motives. He even went along with her when she brought up the Munchausen By Proxy. Maybe her father had died from the flu and she'd cared for him during that time.

You know, Cole, when you keep pointing the finger at someone else, three fingers point back at you. Why are you so intent on pushing suspicion onto Kimberly?

She gasped. What if Cole knew that Kimberly was having an affair with Hector, and he killed him but wants to throw suspicion on Kimberly? She needed to get those bottles.

She rang Cole's phone number.

He answered. "Yes?"

"Cole, what happened to the stuff at Hector's?"

"It was given away, and his personal items were put in storage. Why?"

"I mean, the contents of his kitchen, like the refrigerator?"

"I threw them all in the bins in the back. Why are you asking?"

"Nothing." Christie hung up the phone. It had been Cole who had removed the bottles. Not the Websters. But had he done it on his own, or had Emma or Tyler Webster ordered him to do it? What was worse, Cole now knew she wanted those bottles.

That was a dumb mistake, Christie.

Now to get with Trish and see when they could get those bottles. They couldn't wait.

By the time the pair arrived back at Hector's, the trash cans had been emptied.

"Great." Christie looked around for any place that could hold other bags of trash. "I thought you said the trash doesn't come until after tomorrow?"

"It doesn't. At least I don't think so." Trish dropped her keys in her purse.

"Someone must have come and taken the trash away."

"Sadly, there's nothing that can be done now. I guess that's that."

"We have to find out who took it." Christie strode toward the street and the front of the house. I'm going to talk to that neighbor." As she pointed, the curtain in the window across the street from Hector's once more fell into place.

Trish grabbed Christie's arm. "Listen, you can't just go barging in like a bull in a china shop. I live here. Let me see if I can get any answers from them."

"Probably a good idea." Christie nodded.

"Back in two ticks." Trish walked across the street and knocked on the bright pink painted door. The door cracked open, revealing an older woman spying out. Seeing Trish, she opened the door wider. Christie couldn't hear the conversation, but the woman smiled and waved at Christie, who waved back. In a few minutes, Trish returned.

"All she'll say is that she saw white trucks during the day and a blonde woman taking some bags away."

"Terrific. That doesn't help narrow it down for us. All the Webster team drive white trucks, and of course, Emma and Kimberly are both blonde. Heck, even Shana May is blonde depending on the day. How good do you think her eyesight is for spotting someone?"

"Hmm. That's a good question. I would say fairly good. Why do you ask?"

"She may be the only witness who can testify to who went in and out of that house."

"Oh, that's too bad."

Christie responded. "What?"

"I doubt she's really got a great memory. She called me by some other woman's name."

Christie wiped sweat from her forehead. "Ugh, this heat is something I'm not excited about. I guess we've done all we can do."

"Yes, best to leave it. It was probably heatstroke, like you said." Trish nodded and dug her keys from her purse.

Christie motioned for the pair to get in a vehicle. Once inside the truck with the AC jacked up, she said, "What about my phone though?"

"What about it?" Trish set her bag in her lap and started digging through it.

"I didn't text Hector. So who did and why?"

Trish shrugged. "Maybe your Pop did it."

"Pop barely uses the phone. He certainly doesn't text and he's the one who found my phone." She moved an air vent to blow cold air on her.

Trish pulled a lip gloss from her bag and swiped it across her mouth. "Maybe you forgot you texted Hector."

Christie retorted, "I didn't forget about texting him. I've never texted him."

Trish sighed and threw the gloss back in the bag. "Just trying to help here. I mean things have been a bit crazy. It wouldn't be surprising to do something and forget about it. Where did your dad find your phone?"

Christie adjusted in her seat. "On the ground. By the back of the Jeep."

"Maybe you just dropped it during all the commotion with your dad. Just saying. It could have happened."

"No, I..." Christie thought back to when she'd last seen the phone. Had she just dropped it and not noticed? But she'd walked by the Jeep all the time. No, she would have seen it. The deputy would have seen it. Except...she had moved her Jeep under the tree, so it would stay cooler in the shade.

Trish wiped a corner of her mouth with her finger. "Look, you've been going through a lot. It wouldn't be surprising if you dropped your phone in all the commotion. Or forgot that you'd texted Hector."

"But I didn't. That's one thing I do know for certain."

"Okay."

Trish's "okay" only placed more doubt in Christie's mind. Had she texted Hector and simply forgotten? She'd said she was going to contact the Websters about the accident. But she wouldn't have texted Hector. She certainly wouldn't have had him meet her by the creek.

"Come on. We can figure it out later." Trish waved toward the window of the neighbor's house. "Headed home?"

"No. I'm going to visit some of the new shops on Main Street. Want to join me?"

"Nope, I've got to get Jess to another practice. Thanks for the invite."

After leaving Trish, Christie spent the rest of the day running errands and getting reacquainted with the lovely little town of her childhood. She'd called Pop about catching a movie, but he'd told her to go ahead without him. Arriving home after dark, Christie exited the Jeep and opened the door to see Pop asleep in a chair. She smelled something burning and from the kitchen, a haze of gray smoke twisted into the living area.

Chapter Twelve

"Pop! Pop! Get up! The kitchen's on fire!" He grunted but didn't move. Christie grabbed him up from the chair and hurried him out to the front door. She helped Pop into her vehicle. After moving her car away from the house, she ran around to the back to the kitchen.

The kitchen door stood open, and heavier smoke poured through the opening. Christie couldn't see any fire, but she gingerly opened the screen door. Propping it open, she peeked inside. On the stove, a cast iron skillet churned with thick black smoke. Flames licked the sides.

Christie grabbed a large bag of baking soda from under the sink and scooped a cup out. She carefully sprinkled the baking soda over the area and as the smoke calmed, she poured more of the baking soda into the pan. Grabbing an oven mitt, she placed a cast iron griddle pan on top as a cover. Smoke trickled out the sides, but it looked to be contained. With the pan covered, she turned off the back burner and slid the pan to the side.

Looking around, she saw blackened, soot-covered walls. If she hadn't come home...no, she didn't want to think about it. She choked back a sob. Christie went around to the truck where her father's head lolled to the side. He was still groggy.

"Pop! Pop! Wake up!"

He looked at her through blurry eyes. "What...what's going on?"

"You left a pan with bacon grease burning on the stove. You could have set the house on fire or been killed. What were you thinking?" Her anger boiled over.

"I did no such thing."

"Pop, I barely saved the kitchen. It was minutes, if not seconds, from going up the back of the wall. If that would have happened, the entire place would have gone up in flames." She broke down in tears.

"Ah, girly. Don't go on crying. It's okay." His

words slurred.

"It's not okay, Pop. You could have been killed." She wiped her eyes with the back of her hand. "Pop, look at me. Did you take any medication?"

Christie looked at his pupils. There was definitely some sort of drug in his system.

"Come here, now, darling." He took her in his arms, and she wept quietly on his chest. After she'd composed herself, he held her arms and looked at her. "On my honor, I did not leave that pan on."

She sniffled. "Did you cook bacon today?"

"Yes, but I turned off the stove."

"Maybe you thought you had but left it on or turned it on by accident."

"Or 'ya-Hootie' did it."

Christie moaned. Ever since she was a child, a running family joke had been that when something would happen that no one would fess up to, her father always said it must have been 'ya-Hootie' who had done it. "Pop, be serious."

He moaned and pulled his arm next to his

chest.

"Are you hurt, Pop?"

"Naw. I just must have slept crooked-like. It's just a bit sore, is all."

"Should we take you to the doctor? Did you breathe in any of the smoke?"

He waved her away, and she backed up as he exited the vehicle and stumbled. "I'm all right. No need to fuss." He sat in one of the wooden chairs under the trees.

Christie followed suit and sat in the chair opposite him. "Pop, why didn't you wake up? Didn't you hear the boys barking? Did you take a pain pill?"

"I just got so sleepy all of a sudden. I think I let the dogs out when Marie stopped by."

"Marie came here?"

"Yes. She came over because she wanted to see how you were getting on, and she brought me a piece of pie, too. We had a nice chat, then she left."

"Then you cooked the bacon?"

"Naw. I cooked it earlier." He looked at Christie. "Don't be giving me those looks, Missy. I'm telling you; I didn't leave the stove on."

"You could have forgotten."

"I didn't."

"But you could have."

"I could have. But I didn't. I haven't. I wouldn't."

Christie sighed. They were getting nowhere. "Pop, I'd feel better if you went in for a check-up."

"I don't need to go to no doctors. I'm fine."

"If you're in pain from your shoulder, that's what pain pills are for. But they can make you sleepy. I just need to know if you took one or two. We don't want something to happen where you're asleep."

"I did not take any of them pills."

She rose. "Let's talk about it later. For now, I need to start wiping down the kitchen walls and cleaning up."

Inside the kitchen, she surveyed the damage. Not bad, but it would take some elbow grease. Before she started, she called Trish, but the call went to voicemail. Christie left Trish a phone message, telling her what had happened. She then got Marie's phone number and called her.

"Marie. Hi, it's Christie. Sorry to bother you so late—"

"No problem. You sound upset. Is everything okay?"

"Yes. Well, not exactly. Listen, my Pop said you stopped by earlier."

Marie answered, "I did. I wanted to see how you all are doing after the accident and, well, everything else."

"Pop's doing okay. But here's the reason I'm calling. We had a grease fire in the kitchen and—"

"Oh, no. So sorry to hear that. Are you all okay? Do you need someplace to stay?"

"Thanks. We're fine, and the house is okay. Just some smoke damage in the kitchen that shouldn't be too difficult to fix. That kitchen could use a good painting anyway. From what I can gather, I believe it started from when Pop fried some bacon earlier. He said that he didn't leave the stove on. I'm just trying—"

"I did smell bacon when I arrived, but everything was fine when I got there."

"Did you go in the kitchen?"

"Yes. I went in to get forks to share the pie I brought with me."

What am I missing?

"Just another question, Marie. When you left, were the dogs inside or outside?"

"I think they went outside. They were barking something awful, so I think there must have been an animal around. Your Pop let them outside, and they took off to who knows where. Then, we went out front to the oaks."

"Okay. Well, thanks. Wait. You all weren't in the house when you ate the pie?"

"No. We thought we'd go out front and enjoy the shade and cool breeze."

"Appreciate it. Thanks again. Goodnight."

"Let me know if you need anything. I can paint, too."

"Thanks for the offer."

After they said goodbye, Christie disconnected the call. First Curtis's accident, and now, her father's near-miss. Those were some incriminating coincidences. Yes, both men were elderly. The incidents could be connected or simply things that happened. She rubbed her head and saw her reflection in the kitchen window. She pointed at the reflection, "Hey, you! I could use some help figuring this out."

"Who you talking to?"

Christie screamed. "Pop, don't sneak up on me like that. You scared me to death."

"If everything's okay now, I'm going to watch the news. You coming, 'ya-Hootie?'" He grinned at her and left the kitchen.

She opened the door and stood on the back porch. She heard a crack. Searching the copse of trees, she couldn't see anything.

Probably a deer.

Goosebumps rose on her arms. The feeling of being watched was overwhelming. If someone had intended to burn down the house, there had to be a reason. She was getting close. Unfortunately, she still had no idea who had wanted Hector out of the way or if this was even linked to his death. Christie went inside and turned out the kitchen lights. Searching for any movement, she finally relaxed.

You're being silly

Another crack.

She swiveled around just in time to see a figure astride a horse riding away.

Chapter Thirteen

It was too dark, thanks to only a sliver of waning moon, so Christie couldn't make out the rider. Had they set the fire or simply watched from the trees? The only way they could have gotten on this land was if they had come from the Altgelt homestead. They had to know Curtis was in the hospital.

Christie rushed into the house and grabbed her keys to the Jeep. "Pop, I'll be back in a minute!" She swept past him.

Inside the vehicle, she cranked the engine and shoved the car in reverse. Rocks spit out from under the trees as she did a one-eighty in the drive. Christie slammed on the brake, then shoved the car into drive. She sped off, adrenaline driving her, but reality hit when she got about halfway down the road. Christie slowed the car down and put it in park.

What are you thinking? What do you plan to do once you get there—accost them?

Her head throbbed, and she leaned it on the steering wheel. Her mind raced. What were the real facts?

Fact. Hector was dead, but it could have been heatstroke; simply an accidental death.

Fact. Curtis was hurt, yes, but other than the fence being cut, there was no evidence there, either. Fact. A fire had started in a pan full of grease. Again, this could be accounted for if her Pop had taken medication. Her father was elderly, and he could have easily forgotten to turn off the burner on the stove.

There was nothing menacing about any of it; just a bunch of simple coincidences.

But she was concerned about her father being drugged. He had most likely forgotten that he'd taken a pain pill earlier and then taken another. But that scenario didn't bode well for him being alone right now or in the future.

As for the rider, yes maybe they shouldn't have been on their property, but trespassing didn't mean the person was a murderer. If only she could have gotten a better look at them. Maybe they had smelled the smoke and had come to help, and when they saw that everything was okay, they left.

Christie shifted in her seat and slowly backed the vehicle to a turn-out on the road. Images filled her mind of the girl's trip to Colorado.

You have to forget what happened there. It makes you suspect everyone of bad intentions and murderous thoughts. You're letting your imagination get the best of you.

Yet the nagging thoughts wouldn't stop intruding.

What about my phone? Someone took it and used it to call Hector. What would be the reason for that if not to make me seem culpable in something?

If Hector had seen the text, he would have thought she wanted to talk about her father's accident or selling the property. Hector probably thought she wanted to meet by the creek so her Pop wouldn't be part of the conversation and he didn't know her so he wouldn't have known that she never would have done that.

Returning to the house, she saw her father framed in the light of the door. His figure slumped against the doorjamb, and she could see him cradling the shotgun. She got out of the truck and yelled, "Pop, what are you doing?"

"Now, Christie, you don't think I'd let a girl of mine go off without her ol' Pop to protect her, do you?"

She took the shotgun from him. "Pop, thanks for loving me and making sure I'm all right. What were you planning to do?"

"If you hadn't of come to your senses, I was coming after you." He groaned and sat down on the closest rocking chair. "I'm really tired."

Christie took the shotgun inside and secured it above the door. She returned to the porch and sat in the other chair. "Pop, I think that we need to have a talk."

"Not now. Not today."

"Okay." She patted his hand. They rocked in silence, listening to the cicadas.

"Rain must be on its way."

"We could sure use it," she replied.

"Yep."

The squeak of the chair legs beat out a rhythm, lulling them into silence. Christie gazed at the stars. They were so bright against the deep midnight blue sky. She took in a breath of clean country air. Tears pricked at her eyes. For so many who owned land that went back generations, this life of simple pleasures was being destroyed. She wouldn't let this land become another statistic.

"Pop—"

"I ain't selling."

"Good."

~~~

Another morning. Another miserably hot day ahead. The cicadas had been lying. No rain. She went out to the barn early in the morning before the heat became unbearable and mucked out the stalls. It was hard work, but Christie was used to physical labor, and she needed the outlet. She
~~~

grabbed hay and spread it in the stalls, then filled the water trough. She watched as the foal nuzzled her mother, her tail flicking the flies away. Christie shielded her eyes from the glaring sun as she heard her name called.

"Christie, come in. Breakfast's ready," Trish spoke.

"Be there in a minute." She went over to the boot scraper and ran her soles across the bars. With the bottoms clean, she headed toward the back porch, where she pulled the boots off and slipped into a pair of flip flops.

"Girl, you need a spa day. Look at those nails and toes. Pitiful." Trish poured coffee into Christie's cup. "Does it smell like smoke in here to y'all?"

Christie took a sip of the brew which was black and strong like she liked it. "We had a grease fire in here a few nights ago. Thankfully, I caught it in time."

"Did you call the fire department?"

"No."

"What? That's how people get hurt; trying to

put out fires by themselves."

"I'm sure that's true. But if I had waited, it may have caught the wall behind the stove on fire, and the whole place would have gone up."

Trish smeared some plum jam on her toast and took a bite. " Mmm. I love your jam, Pop."

He grunted and kept eating.

"So, any more thoughts on Hector or Kimberly?"

Christie set her fork down. "I think it was just an accident with Hector. Kimberly may have been having an affair with him. But that's not for me to judge."

"Then, Kimberly gets off, scot free. Again."

"What do you mean?" Christie stared at Trish.

"Don't you ever feel like she has everything handed to her on a silver platter?"

"No. Trish, what's up?"

Pop wiped his mouth with his napkin and stood up. "I'll leave you to it." He went out to the front.

Christie heard the truck start up. "Hold on, Trish. He doesn't need to be driving yet." She rushed out front, yelling, "Pop! Pop!" She waved her hands in the air, and he stopped the truck. She ran over to his window. "Where are you going? Your arm isn't healed. You shouldn't be driving."

"I'm going to see Curtis. I'm a grown man, and no one tells me what I can or can't do, not even you."

"But—"

"No buts." He swiveled to face her better. "I don't give advice, and you can throw mine out, too, but sometimes we're so close to something, we can't see the trees for the forest."

"You mean the forest for the trees?"

"Nope. But you'll have to figure it out on your own." He tipped his hat, and Christie backed away from the truck. She watched as he drove off, then made her way back into the kitchen. Trish stood at the sink, washing up the skillet.

"Thanks for doing that. I appreciate it." Christie wiped down the table and put the condiments in the refrigerator.

"Happy to help." Trish turned the heat on under the skillet to dry it.

Christie stared at the skillet.

"What's up?"

"The skillet."

"What about it?" Trish looked back at the stove.

"My Pop always uses the left front side."

"Okay?"

"You put it on the right side in the front."

Trish cocked her head. "Sorry. I'm not getting your meaning. Do I need to move it over?"

"No." Christie shook her head. "I'm just thinking out loud here." She walked over and put the skillet on the left hand side. Then, she pushed it to the back burner. She stared at the stove.

"Am I missing something here?" Trish looked from the stove to Christie.

"No. Just trying to figure things out."

Trish smiled at Christie. "Girl, I think you are tired. That fire business, along with everything else, has gotten to you. Should we take another horseback ride?"

"I'd love to, but not today. How about a walk over to the creek?"

"Sounds nice."

The pair walked and talked about high school antics, what had been happening in the years since, and Christie shared about the experience in Colorado getting snowed in with a killer college classmate. "That's why I had to take a break. I'm used to death in my profession, but it was the final straw as they say. I needed to get away for a while."

"I'm glad you're home. It's nice having you back here," Trish quipped.

They reached the crest of the hill, then started down the path to the creek. A vehicle was parked at the bottom, close to where Hector's truck had been.

Trish huffed. "The nerve of that woman!"

The two strode toward Kimberly's truck. The woman looked up and wiped her eyes as they approached. "Hi. I just felt the need to come see where..." She stifled a sob.

"Where Hector died?" Trish spat out.

Christie turned and looked at Trish, who bit her lip.

"Kimberly, I—"

"I told you to stay away from Cole."

"What are you talking about? Wait, were you spying on us the other day?"

"I thought Cole was cheating on me, and it turns out I was right!"

Christie stepped forward. "I don't know what you think you saw, but nothing, and I do mean nothing, is going on between me and Cole. Anyway, I think that's a bit like the pot calling the kettle black, don't you think?"

Kimberly pushed her hair back from her heavily made up face. "What's that supposed to mean?"

Trish chimed in. "Hey, let's calm down. We're all friends, remember? How about we all take a breath?"

"You're right," Christie said. She looked around. "Remember when we all used to come down here in the summer?"

Kimberly moved away from the truck and over toward a bank of trees. "We had such fun here. Everyone would bring something to eat and drink, and some nights, we'd have a campfire. It was the best time of my life."

"If stealing people's boyfriends is what you call 'the best times.'," Trish snapped.

"Whoa, there." Christie was stunned by the sudden change in Trish. "What happened to 'let's take a break?'"

Trish and Kimberly glared at each other.

"I have to go." Trish turned on her heel and strode back to the house, leaving Kimberly and Christie behind.

"As always. Trying to get attention and have the last word."

"I don't see—" Christie swatted at a fly.

"Of course, you don't. You never saw her for who she really is." Kimberly turned and faced the creek. "It's really hot. I think I'm going to stick my feet in the water."

"I'll join you and you can tell me more about what you mean."

The pair sat in companionable silence. Finally, Kimberly faced Christie.

"Okay. I do owe you an apology. I did steal

Cole from you in high school. It was wrong, but at the time, I was just hung up on all that head cheerleader, quarterback garbage. I'm sorry."

"Thanks. Yes, back then, it was hurtful, but to be honest, I really prefer having my own space. I don't think I'm the marrying kind."

Kimberly splashed her pink-tipped toes in the water. "I think I've always wanted to be married. I would buy the big books of wedding dresses and envision my wedding day."

"And yet, here you are." Christie moved to a more comfortable position against a tree.

"What's that supposed to mean?"

Christie motioned back to the field. "Hector."

Kimberly shook her head. "I'm sorry. What are you talking about?"

"Do I have to come right out and say it?"

"I guess so, since I haven't a clue what you're talking about." She picked up her shoes and put them back on.

"You were having an affair with Hector."

"What?" Kimberly rose and stood on the creek's bank. "Are you insane? I'd never cheat on

Cole."

"Someone's been having an affair with Hector. We figured out that it was either Emma or you. You both have the same fair coloring, the same build, same hair color..."

Kimberly broke down laughing. "Oh. My. Gosh. Just like I said! You are so blind. Same build, same hair color..." She lifted a perfectly arched eyebrow. "Everyone in town knows that when Mike's away, the cat comes out to play."

Chapter Fourteen

Christie paced back and forth across the yard.

Why? Why? Why?

The question repeated in her mind.

"You're gonna dig a trench with all your pacing back and forth, girlie."

She sighed and joined her father on the porch. "Pop, I have a big decision to make. I don't want to lose a friendship, but I can't let this stand, either. I have to know the truth."

"You'll figure out the best way forward." He stood as a white truck pulled up into the yard. Two people were inside. The Websters.

Geez. If this is how they were before I arrived no wonder Pop is acting as he has.

Tyler strolled up to the porch, and Emma followed. "Mr. Taylor?"

"That's who you're speaking to."

"Emma has informed me that you don't want

to sell any of your property for an easement next to the Altgelt property."

"Correct."

Christie held back a smirk. Her Pop wasn't one to mince words.

"Mr. Taylor, I can certainly understand your hesitation. As such, I've increased the offer for that area of land." He held out a piece of paper, but Pop did not take it, so Tyler then turned and handed it to Christie, who gave it a cursory glance.

Whoa, that's a lot of zeros.

She handed it back to Tyler. "I don't think you understand, Mr. Webster. As my father has told Hector, Cole, Emma and now you, this place is not for sale, nor is any part of it."

Tyler Webster handed the paperwork to Emma, who folded it up and stuffed it into her large purse. "We'll be creating a wonderful development on the Altgelt property, and you can keep your property but have a nice nest egg for your retirement."

Pop rocked back and forth in the chair but said nothing.

Tyler continued. "We'll be closing on the Altgelt property soon."

"Are ya now?" Pop stood and shook his head. "You know what I can't abide? Liars." He shooed the Websters off with a flick of his wrist. "You know you may think I fell off the turnip truck. But I'll tell you this, it certainly wasn't yesterday. Now, get off my property before I sic these dogs on you." Mutt and Jeffrey raised their heads, tails thumping.

Tyler scoffed and said, "I'll take my chances."

"I bet you won't take your chances if I grab my eight gauge."

"Are you threatening us to shoot us?" Emma's eyes widened.

"I don't threaten. You are trespassing on my property. You're threatening me by getting out of that there truck and coming up to my porch."

The pair took a step back.

Pop rose and his voice was calm as he said, "Here's how I see it. Curtis is no more selling his property than I am, so you can just tell those greedy kin of his to crawl back under the rock they came from. I'm not selling you one blade of grass. So, git—and don't come back!"

Emma and Tyler moved toward the truck. "This isn't the end of this."

After they left, Christie spoke to her father. "Pop, do you know for a fact that Curtis isn't selling? I mean, he's hurt pretty badly, and at his age, the property would pass to those boys since they're the only relatives."

"Not to worry. Me and Curtis, we got it all figured out. We talked the other day when I visited him in the hospital. It's all taken care of."

Christie sat back in the rocker. "What did you do?"

"You needn't worry your pretty head over it. Just know it's safe from those buzzards. Now, back to what we were talking about. I feel like you've come to a decision about something, am I right?"

She nodded her head. "Yes, I have to do something, and while I'm not sure I want to, it's the right thing to do."

He nodded. "You know in your heart what you

have to do. The best way to pull off a bandage is to yank it off. It hurts a lot, but it's better that way."

"Okay." Christie picked up her phone and punched in a number she never wanted to call. "I need to speak to Sheriff Clauson, please."

***

"I'm so glad you invited me out for another ride. I needed a break from the house." Trish shifted in her saddle. They'd ridden across the property and were now back by the creek.

"Me, too. With dad's accident, then the fire, it was just a lot to deal with." She dismounted and led Champ over to the water to drink.

Trish followed suit with Scout walking behind her.

"You know, I talked with Kimberly the other day. She apologized for stealing Cole in high school." Christie fed Champ part of an apple.

"Really? That's a shocker." Trish led her horse to the creek. "She always thought she could take whatever she wanted. Do whatever she wanted. She's one of those people who the sun always seems to shine on, ya know?"

"Yes. Remember that time in school with her cat? How she got all that attention after it scratched her? Then, it died?"

"Do I? I hated that cat. It scratched me too, if you remember. I think Kimberly was pulling it away when it scratched her." She sat on the grass. "But who got the attention? Not me! It was always Kimberly."

CRACK. The sound came from the brush pile near them. Trish peered over that way. Christie motioned toward the creek. "Must be a momma deer. Been seeing quite a few lately with their fawns coming down to drink."

Trish nodded, "Yep, lots of deer on the Altgelt place too." She hesitated. "I mean, I'd think there were."

"Makes sense." Picking at a piece of tall grass, Christie quipped, "Back to what you were saying, Kimberly always did get the attention in our group. I would be surprised if she didn't kill that cat, herself. I mean, who could blame her? That cat was mean. Besides, look at all the sympathy she received."

"Yeah. I didn't expect that."

"What?"

"Nothing." Trish leaned back on her elbows, closed her eyes, and lifted her face toward the sun. "Let's not talk about Kimberly."

"Okay." Christie crossed her legs and said quietly, "You know, Cole made a pass at me the other day. I think he wants to leave Kimberly."

Trish shot upright. "What did you say? He made a pass? At *you?*"

"I know, right? I'm so different from Kimberly. She's petite, I'm substantial. She's a blonde, and I'm a brunette. You'd think if he had a type, he would have made a pass at you."

Trish bolted up, and Christie quickly followed, while she continued speaking. "In fact, you and Kimberly, and even Emma Webster, are all similar in looks. From a distance—"

Trish clenched her fists tightly as vitriol poured forth, "I'm not stupid. You can stop your innuendoes."

Christie took a step back. "You were the one having the affair with Hector, not Kimberly, and not Emma. You tried to make it look like it was Kimberly by leaving things you knew she used at his house. You wanted her to look guilty."

"You think you're so smart. I didn't want to kill Hector. I wanted to kill Kimberly!" Her hand flew to her mouth and then she laughed loudly. "Whoops. Didn't mean to say that aloud. Oh, well. Too late now." She laughed hysterically. "Christie, look at your face. I'm kidding, silly. Why would I want to kill anyone?"

Christie kept talking. "Kimberly stole Cole from you. You wanted her out of the picture. Who could blame you with Mike gone all the time and so much responsibility on your shoulders at home."

Trish shook her hands and paced back and forth. "That's right. I've had a hard time. How *could* anyone blame me? I've loved Cole my entire life. I wanted him. First, I had to stop you all from dating in high school. That was easy."

This shocked Christie, but she didn't want to stop Trish from continuing.

"Before I even had a chance, Kimberly

swooped in and grabbed him. That was okay. I had found Mike at the time, but that soon fizzled. He's worthless. So, I waited. I knew they were unhappy and that it would only be a matter of time. But then Kimberly had the girls. I tried to get Cole to think Kimberly was a bad mother, but even that didn't work." She stopped pacing and her eyes narrowed as she spoke.

"Hector was a diversion. That was all. One night Hector told me he and Cole were thinking of starting up their own firm. It was Kimberly's idea. He said they'd found a great opportunity for them in the Austin area. She was going to take him away from me again!" Trish spat out, her fists clenching again. "I couldn't let her take Cole. He was close to leaving her, then, we would be together. Mike's gone all the time. He makes good money in the oil field, or I would have left him sooner. No, I had to stop her. I knew what to do."

"You've always been clever."

Be quiet. Let her talk.

Trish glanced at her like she'd just realized

Christie was there. "Yes, I'm smart, all right. Kimberly drinks these stupid electrolyte drinks. She says they give her energy. I didn't know she'd gotten Hector hooked on them." She shrugged. "I mean, how was I to know, right?"

Christie nodded but said nothing.

"But that was even better. Now, I could really get rid of Kimberly. I started rumors, knowing they'd get back to Hector, by telling Marie about Cole possibly starting a business without Hector. That's why he and Kimberly were fighting in the parking lot. Marie's a huge gossip and I knew she'd confront Hector as soon as she could. Then, I planted things of Kimberly's at his house and started the rumors about the affair. We look enough alike that people would easily believe she was the woman they'd seen with Hector."

An idea formed in Christie's mind. "Like the woman who lives across from Hector."

"Lived. Past tense. Poor dear. But when you said she was the only witness, well, I couldn't let her say something, now, could I? I told her when I went to her door that you loved that color pink but were too embarrassed to ask about the shade. Later, I took her a pie—from you, of course. But I had to get a pie pan from your house. You know, just in case someone decided she died of something other than old age."

Christie felt her stomach clench. She'd sealed a woman's death warrant. "So you started the fire in our kitchen?"

Trish jerked back. "What kind of a person do you think I am? Of course not." She glared at Christie. "I thought we were friends."

She's insane.

"We are. I was just trying to figure out the fire. You know, loose ends."

Trish took a step toward Christie. "Ahhh, Christie. I always thought we were BFF's, but Cole making a pass at you? You shouldn't have told me that." She took another step.

"What are you, five-two? You think you're going to fight me?" Christie asked.

"Oh, I have something that makes our height not an issue." Trish reached down and pulled a knife from her boot. She switched it open.

"We are friends. We can work this out." Christie held up her hands and tried to back away.

Trish advanced. "I wish we could, but unfortunately, you're going to have a terrible freak accident."

Christie took another step back. "Plus, that has your prints all over it, and I told Pop I was with you, so it's going to point to you."

"Don't worry. As I said...a tragic accident." Tears sprung to her eyes. "See, I'm already heartbroken." A smile quickly replaced the tears. "Drama class, remember it? I took more classes in college, too. They came in so handy."

"You're crazy!" Christie yelled.

Trish lunged at Christie with the knife. Christie twisted to the right, and the knife hit her upper arm. In a quick movement, Christie grabbed the fleshy part of Trish's hand and pressed down with all her might. Trish fell to her knees, screaming out in pain.

"Drop it!" Christie shouted.

The sound of voices and men running across the field kept Christie upright and pressing on

Trish's hand.

One of the men said, "You can let go now." Someone removed her hand, and she heard the deputy's voice on the radio.

"Need Ambulance. Taylor Ranch."

Another voice answered and the deputy replied, "Suspect in custody."

She looked down at her arm and the red that was spreading down her sleeve. She raised her hands and stared at them as they shook. Her body trembled.

I'm going into shock.

She dropped to the ground and bent her head to her knees. She began counting her breaths.

One... Two...

Her mind knew what to do but her body and emotions wouldn't listen. She broke down sobbing. Her arm throbbed with pain, but her heart was broken.

A voice carried across the expanse of pain and sorrow. "Step back. That's my girl."

"Daddy," she cried out.

Chapter Fifteen

"We the jury pronounce the defendant guilty."

Guilty.

Guilty.

Guilty.

The words kept repeating in Christie's mind. How could her friend—the one she'd known practically all her life—be guilty of murder? It was a surreal feeling. Even more strange was getting a phone call from the jail where Trish was being held. After the jury had pronounced Trish guilty of manslaughter, the judge had handed down a sentence of ten years. With good behavior, Trish could be out in a few years. The question was why would she possibly want to see Christie?

Driving up to Kerrville seemed to take forever. After going through the security protocols, Christie found herself in a room with a bank of phones. Glass partitions separated them. Trish picked up her phone, and Christie followed suit. They said nothing and only stared at one another.

After a while, Trish sighed. "I'm sorry." She tipped her head. "About your arm. I went insane. I was about to lose everything. My son, my home, my husband…"

Trish had ended up losing more than that, she'd lost her freedom and destroyed lives around her in addition to her own. She roughly wiped the tears from her eyes. "Anyway. I'm being transferred tomorrow to the state, um, facility and I want to give you something." This wasn't something Christie expected. She waited as Trish continued, "I want you to have my horses. Mark is filing for divorce and selling our house. Poor Jess."

Christie shook her head. Trish had brought this on her son, not her husband.

"Is Jess going to live with his dad in Midland?"

"He doesn't have a choice. He has to go with his father. But it's going to be so hard on him. And with only one year left in high school. His coach said he had a great chance at a football scholarship." She placed her palm on the glass. "Unless...someone lets him stay here and finish out the year."

Christie shook her head. "You certainly don't mean at Pop's place?"

"Oh, would you? It would mean the world to me, Christie."

"No. No." Christie sat back in her seat. "Pop is too old. He can't handle a teenage boy."

"But *you* could."

"I think you're forgetting. I'm only here for a bit. I have a life, elsewhere."

"Doing what? Caring for dying people? How is that a life?"

"I really help them. And their families." Christie fumed.

Trish nodded. "I'm sure you do, and that you're really good at it. But aren't you ready for something different? Don't you want to come home?"

"We don't have the room, even if that was a

possibility. I've been sleeping on the couch because the back room isn't livable until it's been cleaned out and repairs are done in it."

"I could talk to Mike. He's always respected Mr. Taylor. I know he understands that Jess will be by himself while he's out in the oilfields. How much better if he could stay in Comfort where he has friends, someone can watch over him, and he can finish his last year at school? He could go up to Midland on breaks to see his dad."

Christie felt the pull.

No. You're not getting involved. But poor Jess. He doesn't deserve this. He's a good kid.

Trish smiled. "I can see you're torn. Don't do it for me. Do it for Jess. Plus, he's an old pro with the horses. He can help you around the property, too. He loves working with his hands."

Jess was a strapping young man—over six foot with lots of muscle. It would definitely benefit Pop to have Jess there to help around the house with chores.

"Listen, how about you think about it? Talk with Pop about it. See what he thinks. In the meantime, Jess is staying with his friend's family. And, of course, Mike would pay a monthly stipend for Jess so you wouldn't be spending any of your money on him." A guard came up and touched Trish's shoulder. "Well, looks like my fans are calling. Please. Think about it." She stood and re-placed the phone.

Christie stared at the blank space. She'd been surprised that Trish would give her the horses, but Mike would certainly sell them. He couldn't care for them being away in the oilfields. Christie loved horses, and she and Champ had formed a bond in their short time together, but she had no place for them where she lived. Certainly, Pop was in no physical state to care for the horses. Jess could care for the horses without a problem, but other issues would be involved. She had a lot to think about and a trip back to Comfort to ponder everything.

But aren't you ready for something differ-ent? Don't you want to come home?

Truth be told, Pop wasn't getting any younger. There was no telling how long he would be around. The incident with the stove the other night had increased her fear of him living on such a big property alone. Plus, she knew the Websters wouldn't stop their constant attempts to acquire the property. The sight of Curtis passed out in the field came to her mind. That could have been Pop.

Conflicting emotions pulled at her. She had made no progress or decision by the time she pulled up in front of the old place. Pop came out onto the porch, waving a dishtowel with his uninjured arm.

She slid out of the truck and was greeted with something that sounded like "Deetjet?" He wiped the towel across his forehead. "Hotter than a—"

"No. I haven't eaten yet."

They ate German potato salad, coleslaw, and smoked brisket. When they finished, Christie told Pop to go outside and that she'd clean the dishes. After making quick work of the washing up, she joined him on the porch. A breeze from the ceiling fan cooled off the day's heat and made the area bearable. They rocked in silence.

"You know, girly? I been thinking 'bout what

you said. I done feel sorry for that kid, Jess. But I'm just too old and set in my ways to have another young-un to bring up." He pointed to a spot out across the field.

"That area would be a good spot for a swimming hole."

Christie turned to him with a surprised look. "Um, what brought that up?"

Pop raised his hand and stopped her from continuing. "Not for me. Ya know, I was thinking that, when I die, you will need to sell this place, and if we put in a pool and a nice little house behind it, you could stay there, ya know, when ya come home to visit and such."

"For visits?" Christie made a face and raised her eyebrows.

"Yep. Course, if we did build it, it could be a place for poor Jess to stay, too. But he'd need someone here more full-time like."

Christie bit at her lip. "Full-time like?"

"I can't do it, but I wouldn't mind the help, that's for sure." He glanced over at her, pushed his chin up and pursed his lips. "What do you think, darlin?"

"I think it's time I moved home."

~~~
~~~

For more information on book launches and reader giveaways, join my newsletter at www.vikkiwalton.com.

~~~

If you enjoyed this book, please leave a review on your favorite retailer site.
~~~

Other Books by Vikki Walton

Backyard Farming Series

Chicken Culprit

Cordial Killing

Honey Homicide

Taylor Texas Series

Death Takes A Break

Death Makes A Move (2020)

Death Stakes A Claim (2020)

Death Bakes A Plan

Nonfiction Books

Work Quilting: Piece Together Diverse Income Streams, Live an Insanely Awesome Life!

The Smart Women's Guide to Travel